cute book some funny parts boy meets girl book +8

"You are a scoundrel, sir."

Lucy politely answered Lord Roderick's enquiry as to why she had agreed to pose as his betrothed only to take him into such aversion.

The epithet vastly amused him. "What is that to the purpose, my love? No woman ever disliked a man for being a scoundrel. In my experience, she likes him the better for it."

Here Lucy saw her opportunity to teach him the lesson she had come to impart. "You are mistaken. *I*, for example, do not like a scoundrel. I cannot esteem a man who makes love to a great many women at once and then, when they quite naturally think of matrimony, invents an engagement to fob them off."

"You appear to have made a study of me, my love," he said with some amusement. "Perhaps you do not despise me as much as you say." On that, he reached for her hand, which had rested in her lap.

"Sir, I warn you," she said in a low, serious voice.

"On the contrary, my dear," he answered smoothly. "I warn you. I mean to teach you exactly what it is to be engaged to a scoundrel."

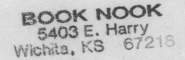

LUCY'S SCOUNDREL

BARBARA NEIL

Harlequin Books

TORONTO • NEW YORK • LONDON
AMSTERDAM • PARIS • SYDNEY • HAMBURG
STOCKHOLM • ATHENS • TOKYO • MILAN

Published January 1991

ISBN 0-373-31141-9

LUCY'S SCOUNDREL

CHAPTER ONE

Crossed In Love

LUCY BLEDSOE consulted her guidebook, then looked up at the cathedral spires to admire the old Mapildon tower. She could not help noticing that as she observed the tower, she herself was observed.

Two of the women of Canterbury stood nearby whispering, and from their frequent looks in her direction, she deduced that they were whispering about her. Because she was known for carrying herself with the greatest elegance, and because she wore the smartest of deep blue dresses, she could not imagine that her appearance should inspire such blatant stares. She immediately glanced down to see whether her hem was muddy but found, upon inspection, that it was clean as new. Therefore, she put her hand to her bonnet, thinking its feather might have drooped, but found it as sturdy as she could have wished. Lucy could find nothing at all out of the way in her appearance and was therefore puzzled as to why the two women should be whispering about her.

Lady Philpott came out of the cathedral, exclaimed bitterly against the brightness of the sunshine, and remarked to Lucy, "I have had enough splendour for one morning. Let us go to the shops. I should like to find a card of lace, and if it is not too expensive, I shall buy it.''

Leaving the cathedral precinct, they walked toward the High Street. Lucy looked back to see the two women following her with their eyes. She might have remarked upon their fixed stares had not Lady Philpott suddenly uttered a loud objection to the tangle of purple buddleia which spread its leafy vine like a net along their path. The flower's strong, sweet fragrance inspired her ladyship to lament the Whiggish tendency to allow Nature to grow as it liked, without discipline or decorum.

In the course of this lecture, Lucy became aware of three ladies on the other side of the High Street near the linen draper's shop. They said not a word but closely watched the progress of her walk. It was not until Lucy stared boldly back at them that the ladies desisted from their open gawking. Baffled by such behaviour, Lucy interrupted her companion's flow of criticism to ask, ''Why is it, do you suppose, that the townsfolk stare at me? What can they mean by such looks?''

Lady Philpott replied, ''The rustics must have something to look at, I daresay. There is nothing else to occupy them in such a sleepy town.''

Lucy was forced to accept this explanation. Sighing, she said, ''I wish they would not stare. I had thought to find a little quiet and peace here in Canterbury.''

''If you want my opinion,'' said her ladyship, who always gave her opinion whether it was wanted or not, ''Canterbury offers far too much quiet and peace. There are no gentlemen hereabouts. I should not be surprised to learn that every eligible gentleman in the county has gone off to fight the war. You saw what happened last night at Queenscroft. Lady Roderick could not even make up four couples to dance, except for the married ones, but they do not count. I wish it had been otherwise, for your sake, dear girl. I do wish Lady Roderick's son had been there. Lord Roderick is excessively eligible and is said to be devilishly handsome to boot.''

Lucy smiled and replied, ''I did not regret the scarcity of partners. I did not wish to dance.''

Lady Philpott treated her to a gentle scold. ''I hope you are not thinking of giving up dancing on account of that dreadful man in Bath. Young ladies who pine after such gentlemen are sure to spoil their complexions and yours is too rosy to be spoilt. You must put him out of your mind. As I have told you countless times, my dear girl, a young woman should never love where there is no profit.''

''I had very great profit, my lady. I learned a lesson, and I escaped the clutches of a scoundrel. What more could one ask?''

''A vast deal more, dear girl. Lessons are all very well, but they are tedious things, and spinsterhood is expensive. Every young woman was formed for dancing, falling in love and marrying a husband who will keep her in some style.''

Because she found Lady Philpott's views on marriage highly entertaining, Lucy asked, ''But what happens after a woman marries? It almost seems as though a wife has nothing left to do once she has caught her wealthy quarry.''

''Of course a wife has things to do! What an absurd idea! I know that I was always occupied with shopping. I was required to spend a vast deal of time poking about in shops until I was quite exhausted. Not in Canterbury, however. One cannot call what one does on this High Street 'shopping.' One shops in London. One shops in Bath. I hardly know what one does here." Lady Philpott's ample cheeks had grown red during this heated defense of wives.

"Lady Roderick appears to like the neighbourhood well enough," said Lucy. "She has lived here many years."

"I have the highest regard for Lady Roderick and am thankful she invited us to stay at Queenscroft, but I do not know how she contrives to keep from perishing with boredom in such a place. It is no wonder Lord Roderick declines to visit his mother."

"Is there nothing for a wife to do besides shopping?" Lucy asked. She was not a great shopper and preferred touring cathedrals to amassing buttons and bonnet ribbons.

"Some wives go so far as to give their husbands children," declared her ladyship. "I have heard that children are a great joy, when they do not positively break one's heart. Lord Philpott and I were not blessed with progeny, which is why I am at leisure to look after you in your hour of darkness."

As Lucy smiled at this generosity, they reached the millinery shop. Leaving Lucy at the door, her ladyship stepped inside, where she examined a pretty checked muslin. Hearing that its price was seven shillings a yard, she entered into a dispute with the proprietor, whom she accused of extortion.

Lucy, who did not relish disputes with tradesmen, occupied herself with peeking in the window of a confectioner's shop. Suddenly, behind her, she heard the name of Sir Vale Saunders. With a start, she glanced around to see two well-dressed ladies engaged in earnest conversation. Hearing that all too familiar name had given Lucy a jolt. A further shock awaited her, however, for she also caught the words, "Poor girl crossed in love."

A moment before, she had intended to enter the confectioner's to purchase a bit of angelica for Lady Roderick. Now, having heard what she had heard, she stood still, unable to move. She forgot entirely about the angelica as it came to her all at once why the townspeople stared and whispered when she walked by. She had not been one week in Kent, and already her history was known throughout the neighbourhood. They all knew she had gone to Bath and fallen in love with Sir Vale Saunders. They all knew she had been disappointed. And now they took the opportunity to gossip about her and, worse, to pity her. She felt her face grow hot with mortification.

As soon as Lady Philpott came outside, Lucy expressed her desire to return at once to Queenscroft. Walking at a good pace, they soon left the High Street behind. Lucy composed herself and enquired, "How is it, my lady, that the townsfolk know what passed at Bath?"

"They do not know any such thing. It is none of their business."

"I am afraid they do know. What is more, they stare at me as though I were a figure out of a tragedy."

"My dear, these country clots do not know any better than to stare at an elegant young woman dressed in the latest fashion. You have seen the shops. You know what they are. Naturally, the rustics are reduced to staring at strangers."

"But I overheard one of them mention Sir Vale Saunders."

"Good heavens!" cried Lady Philpott, putting a hand to her cheek. She looked at Lucy in consternation.

"And I heard another whisper the words 'crossed in love.'"

"This is monstrous! How dare they know of all that you have suffered! How dare they speak of it!"

"Lady Philpott, did you mention it to anyone?"

"Only the vicar's wife, my dear girl, but she took her oath never to breathe a word."

Shaking her head, Lucy sighed. "It appears she did breathe a word."

For some time, Lady Philpott frowned in thought. Finally, she waved her richly gloved hand in a gesture of contempt, saying, "I ought never to have brought you here, dear girl. My intention was to find you a husband, as I promised your worthy father I would. But all we have found is dreary churches, villainous shopkeepers and ogling provincials. I vow, my neck is stretched out of its socket from all the gawking at towers, and I shall be with pockets to let if the tradesmen hereabouts have their way. And for what? For nothing. There are no husbands to be found anywhere."

Lucy regarded her companion affectionately, saying, "You are very good to wish to get me a husband, but I am perfectly content without one, I assure you."

Her ladyship returned Lucy's look with one of heartfelt sympathy. "Dear girl, you are too elegant and well bred to make a great fuss or permit yourself to languish, but you cannot hoodwink me. I know that you were greatly affected by Sir Vale's perfidy. Therefore, I am determined to find you a husband, if we can unearth an eligible one, as that is the best cure I know for a broken heart.''

''But my heart is perfectly whole, I assure you, and I do not wish to marry a gentleman who has nothing to recommend him but his eligibility.''

''A woman dares not ask for more in these times of scarcity,'' said her ladyship.

''I require a man of character.''

''Pooh! If you are going to insist upon a man of character, you may as well resign yourself to spinsterhood.''

Laughing, Lucy said, ''You are severe on the male sex.''

''Not at all. I think the gentlemen are precious dears. The world would be a prodigiously tiresome place without them. But for character, you must go to females. You cannot look for such a commodity in men.'' As if to emphasize the truth of her declaration, her ladyship opened her parasol with a snap.

''I cannot agree,'' Lucy said. ''My brother is a good man, and I have met one or two others.''

''There will always be the exceptions to any rule. But I should have thought that Sir Vale taught you what men were made of when he broke your heart. They are a different species from women. They feel less and demand more. They are ruled by whims, like children, and adjust their principles accordingly.''

''I am surprised to hear you speak so cynically. You were happy with Lord Philpott, were you not?''

''I was indeed. The reason we were so happy, however, is that I expected nothing in the way of character from him. I was content to shop and to be a ladyship.''

Although Lucy's recent disappointment in love had shaken her, she could not share Lady Philpott's cynicism with regard to men and marriage. Nor did she dwell on thoughts of husbands, as her ladyship did. While her companion scouted the town for eligible gentlemen, Lucy occupied herself with exploring the ruins of Caesar's fortifications. She took pleasure in picturing Canterbury as it must have appeared in the Middle Ages, with its glorious cathedral, gates and shrines. She conjured up images of Chaucer's pilgrims and visited the birthplace of Christopher Marlowe. To her mind, these were charms exactly calculated to help mend a broken heart. Unfortunately, gossip and stares promised to spoil these charms. With heartfelt regret, Lucy began to think she would be forced to leave Canterbury very soon.

AS SOON AS THE LADIES returned to Queenscroft, they separated, the elder to repair to her chamber where she might scrutinize the ravages wrought by the summer sun on her complexion, the younger to take up a piece of work she had begun in a small sunny parlour. From her cosy vantage point on the window seat, Lucy looked out upon the lawn, across which lay marble steps leading to an expansive rose garden. Partial to roses, Lucy was tempted to pay a visit to the garden. Having set aside her embroidery, she stood and would have started out at once to see the roses, had not the footman entered to announce a visitor.

"Sir Vale Saunders," the servant intoned.

Feeling for the cushion of the window seat, Lucy sat down again. To compose herself, she took a breath, then assumed an expression that she hoped would mask the thudding in her throat. As she awaited Sir

Vale's entrance, she felt like Anne Boleyn awaiting the executioner.

He looked very fine in a coat of deep red with a velvet collar. His cravat lay in perfect folds, and he sported faun pantaloons. The smile he flashed when his eyes fell on her made her heart a drum. Deferentially, he drew near, saying, "I see that Kent agrees with you, Miss Bledsoe. My compliments."

She permitted herself a quick glance at his face, then looked away, nodding in acknowledgement of his greeting. The admiration with which he addressed her was too open to be ignored. She dared not look at him again, knowing that if she did, she might permit herself to hope. Nor did she trust herself to speak. At any attempt to form the least syllable, her voice was sure to tremble.

"May I sit?" he enquired respectfully.

Another brief nod told him he might.

Instead of sitting in the chair that stood at some distance, he fetched it so that he might sit opposite her. This gesture rendered Lucy distinctly uneasy, for it would now be difficult to avoid his eyes when he addressed her.

"What an odd town Canterbury is," he began.

Ordinarily such a curious observation would have served to make her question him further. However, she thought it best not to engage him closely in conversation but simply to wait until he had spoken his piece and then permitted her to breathe again by going away. "Yes" was all she replied.

"I am stared at wherever I go. The townsfolk address me by name, though I never met any of them before in my life."

Having been stared at herself, Lucy sympathized with Sir Vale's wonder, but she did not say so.

Seeing her silent, he went on, "I caused quite a stir at the inn when I arrived yesterday. Everybody appeared to know who I was."

Lucy's blue eyes met his. She coloured, realizing that all of Canterbury had learned of his arrival well before she had and that the villagers, knowing what they knew of her disappointment in love, had probably anticipated this meeting. There was little hope, she saw, of her ever walking the High Street of the town again without provoking speculation and whispers.

"You did not happen to mention me to anyone, did you?" he asked with an appealing smile.

Her chin high, she replied, "Why should I mention your name to strangers? I never expected to set eyes on you again."

Bowing his head, he answered, "There is no reason whatever why you should mention me to your neighbours. Indeed, there is no reason why you should speak to me at all or even think of me, or permit me to see you today." Then, looking at her earnestly, he added, "I only hoped you would."

In spite of herself, she was moved. When she met his eyes this time, it was with a softer expression than she had allowed herself to display earlier.

Seeing the warmth of her blue eyes, the satin of her cheeks, the delicate curl of her honey-coloured hair, he was moved in his turn to take her hand.

"Heaven help me, Lucy," he whispered hoarsely, "I have done a terrible thing."

When she withdrew her hand, he recaptured it and put it to his lips. "I can think of nothing but what I have lost, what I have carelessly thrown away."

She regarded him in some surprise. A month before, Sir Vale Saunders had been the most unrepentant of gentlemen. This change in him could not fail to make her wonder what other changes he would reveal.

"You do not ask," he said sorrowfully, "what it is that I have lost, what precisely I have thrown away. Knowing your goodness and modesty, I cannot wonder at it. You are the very last creature to suspect that the answer is *yourself*."

Lucy turned to gaze out the window so that he would not see her eyes fill. But when he placed his hands on her cheeks, she was compelled to face him once more. For a time, they stared at one another, Lucy searching for a way to comprehend this turnabout in the man, Sir Vale awaiting her verdict in an agony of suspense.

At last, Lucy smiled ruefully. "You have come here to flatter me, Sir Vale. A month's separation has deluded you into thinking you love me. Perhaps I ought to remind you that you never did before."

Removing his hands reluctantly, he stood and paced. "You have every reason to doubt me. I was cruel, unforgivably cruel." Then, with an abrupt turn so that he looked at her with pleading eyes, he added, "If it is any consolation, I harmed myself more than I harmed you. You appear to have recovered wonderfully. Indeed, it is not very flattering to my pride to see just how quickly you have forgotten me."

For an instant, Lucy closed her eyes, thinking that if he knew the truth, he would be as flattered as it was possible for a human creature to be. With an effort, she contrived to smile again and say, "I do not doubt you should have been pleased if I had broken my heart over you."

Pain crossed his face, so that she was sorry she had said anything so light. In a flash, he was on his knee before her, saying, "If you believe nothing else, believe that I would not wish you to suffer a particle of what I have suffered, do suffer, will always suffer."

Overwhelmed by this declaration, Lucy endeavoured to appear in command of her emotions. "Please do get up, Sir Vale. You will soil your coat and your valet will blame me for it."

When he saw that she was gently quizzing him, he returned her smile and stood again. "Do you wish me to leave you?" he said, clearly hoping to hear her say no.

"You cannot make such astounding pronouncements, and then leave me without any explanation. If you wish to oblige me, please sit down again and tell me what has happened to bring on such an unexpected reversal."

He sat. After a pause, he said, "It is this in a nutshell: I am in love with you."

Exaltation welled up in her, so that it took enormous force of will to quell the desire to touch his cheek.

"The reason I have come to Canterbury is to tell you that."

As calmly as she could, she replied, "Then I am glad you have come."

"Can you forgive me?" he asked.

"Of course I can." She watched him as he took her hand in his, and this time she did not draw it away.

"And can you love me again?"

"Of course I can," she repeated. "I'm afraid I never stopped."

Throwing his head back, he exhaled, like a man given a reprieve from the executioner's block. He stood, pulled her up and placed his finger under her chin so that he might look at her face. "Of course you love me," he said, and kissed her. As her arms went round his neck and the mingled sounds of crying and laughter punctuated their embrace, he murmured, "Oh, Lucy, I have been so miserable."

"That is all to be forgotten now," she instructed, luxuriating in his embrace. "I shall make you deliriously happy. So joyful shall you be from this moment forward that the town will take you for a simpleton."

He held her at arm's length to admire her. Then, sweeping her up in his arms, he spun her around. Before he returned her to the carpeted floor, he kissed her again. "Yes, I shall be happy at last."

"Oh, you must not be too happy," she said with a smile that glowed. "Happy husbands are not at all the fashion."

Slowly, he set her down. For an instant, he frowned at her. Then he walked to a table where he opened a Sèvres box to inspect it. "I thought you knew," he said.

"Knew what?"

He shut the box with a snap. "That I am already married. I felt certain you knew. It was announced in the *Times*."

Lucy followed him, staring in disbelief. "I did not know."

He pondered the implications of this new wrinkle. At first, he appeared annoyed, then sceptical, then hopeless, then irritated. Finally, in a voice empty of emotion, he said, "Of course you didn't know. It was absurd of me to imagine you did." Setting down the box, he put his hand to his temple.

Anger blocked her tears, so that she shot at him in a strong voice, "I should never have kissed you, had I known. You must realize that. You know me too well to think otherwise."

He shrugged. "I hoped you had changed your views on these matters. I hoped you would love me enough to be sensible."

Walking to the fireplace, she pulled the bell. "Good day to you, Sir Vale."

He went to her and, taking her by the arm, said intensely, "You *do* love me, you know. It is foolish to pretend you don't. And now I've decided that I love you as well, we may amuse ourselves, don't you see? What is the harm in pleasing ourselves, Lucy? There is so little joy in life; why may we not seize what we can?"

She stared coldly at his hand on her arm until he removed it. At the appearance of the servant, she directed in a low voice, "Please show Sir Vale to his carriage and instruct Merkle that he is never to admit this gentleman to my presence again."

The footman's brow elevated, for despite her quiet tone, she spoke with a regal air of command.

Sir Vale sighed. "You disappoint me, Lucy. I would have made you many handsome gifts. Moreover, I would have entertained you hugely. You know I would."

She approached him with more ferocity than the servant had ever witnessed in that elegant young lady. "If you do not leave at once, I shall be forced to inform your bride and her father that you insist upon paying me unwelcome attentions."

At this, he blanched. "There is no need for that," he murmured hurriedly and went to the door, which the footman held wide for him. Taking one last look at Lucy, Sir Vale declared, "It really is a pity" and was gone.

Her fists tight, her breath coming fast, Lucy had to agree that it *was* a pity—a pity she had held her fury in check, a pity she had behaved in ladylike fashion instead of giving him the reproofs he deserved, a pity she had not hit him across his smug, handsome face, a pity she had been taken in by him yet again. Oh, would she never learn?

CHAPTER TWO

A Canterbury Tale

THE CONSERVATORY at Lever Combe was a south-ward room that in daylight overlooked a purple-and-yellow flower garden. As it was night, not a lupin nor a rose could be seen from the tall windows. Nevertheless, Lord Roderick, fourth Earl of Silverthorne, crossed the room in search of the garden door. He walked slowly because he carried only a small candle. No sooner had he found the door than he was stopped by a breathless voice in the dark saying, "I've come to be with you, my lord. Please do not send me away."

Looking round, he tried to see who was speaking. He inhaled her scent and heard the tap of her satin slippers before he saw the bright eyes of Miss Miranda Crowther-Biggs.

"What the devil are you doing here?" he asked.

"You sent for me."

"When I send for a beautiful young lady, I make it a rule to remember it. I remember no such summons in your case."

He heard her giggle. "You are droll, sir. You know very well you sent for me. I saw you watching me in Lady Knatchbull's saloon. You sent for me with your eyes."

He smiled. "Now that you mention it, I suppose I did. But you cannot stay. Your mama will wonder where you are and send out a search party. If she finds you here, she will not be greatly pleased with either of us."

"Oh, but she will be, for you are the most eligible gentleman at Lever Combe, and Mama says that the purpose of coming to a country house in summer is to meet eligible gentlemen and to get one of them for a husband."

"Your mama is versed in the ways of country houses in summer, I see, but still, I cannot believe she would like to see you risk your reputation, even in such a noble cause."

"Bother my reputation. I've come to be with you. Would you like to kiss me?" she asked.

His lordship moved nearer. He thought Miss Crowther-Biggs a silly girl, a thorough-going flirt, and the most tiresome female he had had the misfortune to meet since the end of the London Season, but as a devout believer in the philosophy that every kiss a man refuses is one he never gets, he answered in the affirmative.

Setting his candle on a table, he studied her in preparation for the kiss. She presented him with a smooth cheek. Laughing, he said, "I shall have to teach you that kissing is not the art of schoolboys," and turned her face to him. Deliberately, he kissed her on the lips. She gasped at first and struggled to break free. At last, sensation overcame surprise and she ceased to squirm. Limply she hung in his arms until he saw fit to release her. She swayed a little on her feet and gazed at him in a seeming trance.

"Are you quite well, Miss Crowther-Biggs?" he enquired. Reaching for the candle, he held it up to her face. At the sight of her large eyes and open mouth, he smiled. It had been a long time since he had kissed a virgin. Now he recollected why. The lovesickness of a maiden paled beside the gratitude of a widow or a wife.

"I shall go at once and tell Mama," the young lady said. "She will want to know that we are engaged."

"My dear Miranda, I don't recall asking for your hand."

"But you kissed me."

"And I would do it again if I did not fear that you would jump to the conclusion that we were actually married. Even at your scandalously young age you must be aware that a kiss does not constitute an engagement."

"But you do wish to become engaged to me, don't you?"

He smiled pleasantly. "Nothing would give me greater joy, naturally. But alas, I am prevented."

"What can prevent you? Mama says you are rich and eligible and your own master."

"Your mama should not have said 'eligible.' You see, the truth is that I am already engaged."

Another gasp brought the girl's hand to her mouth in horror. "That's dreadful."

"It's more dreadful than you know. I am betrothed to a young woman in Canterbury, a young woman I abhor. She knows what my feelings are but will not release me from the promise."

"You must not marry her if you do not love her. It is immoral."

"The first wish of my heart is, of course, to avoid doing anything immoral. Yet I dare not jilt her. My mother, alas, takes the girl's part and will not have it."

"Lady Roderick must be a perfect beast!" she exclaimed. "I cannot comprehend such a mama. Mine would never force me to marry anyone I abhorred. She wishes me to be happy."

Plaintively, he said, "You are fortunate in your choice of mothers. Mine, on the other hand, insists on prudence; I must marry the young woman whose lands lie adjacent to our family's."

"Prudence!" she cried. "I do not give a snap of the finger for prudence! To be engaged where you do not love—it is insupportable."

Producing a sigh that seemed to come from the depths of his soul, he answered, "At my time of life, a man grows accustomed to the insupportable. What is intolerable is the emptiness. There are times when it fairly overpowers me, when all life's luxury and indulgence leave me quite hollow. At such moments, the future appears to promise nothing but unrelieved tedium. The nightingale might sing his chirping little heart out and never cheer me; the sun might beat bravely down on my hatless pate and fail to warm me." This soliloquy done, he observed its effect upon the young lady. He had the pleasure of seeing her so moved that she laid her hand on his arm. "I am very sorry," she said.

"On the other hand," he said, "the kiss of a beautiful young lady sometimes manages to fill the void in my heart."

"Then you must kiss me again," she said earnestly, and he would have done so, except that he was interrupted by the sound of footsteps in the gallery.

In another moment, Owen Hunt came into the conservatory. A flaxen-haired gentleman of the same age as his lordship, he bore a brightly lit candelabrum and a look of consternation. "I've been sent to find you," he said.

"Oh," cried Miranda, "is my mama looking for me?"

For the first time, Hunt noticed Miranda. "Good God!" he exclaimed. "What are you doing here?" Then, looking from his lordship to the young lady, he blushed crimson, for he knew precisely what Miss Crowther-Biggs was doing there: the same thing that ladies young and old did there—and everywhere Lord Roderick happened to go. He murmured, "I had not expected to find you here, Miss Crowther-Biggs. You, of all people!"

"Owen," said the earl, "will you kindly take the young lady to her mama? She has no candle and I fear she may lose her way in the house."

"I should be delighted to return her to the safety of her mother, but—" and here his voice lowered to a nervous whisper "—I must have a word with you, Roderick. It is urgent." He glanced at the girl several times.

"I see that you are in one of your apoplectic moods," said his lordship, smiling. "Very well then, speak, good friend."

With a pained look at Miranda, the young man said, "I cannot speak here. We are not alone."

His lordship nodded, having guessed by Owen's dithers that he carried a message of an intimate nature from a lady. "Tell me, do you come with a message for me?"

"Yes."

"Then you will kindly tell whoever sent the message that you did not find me. Now, you and the young lady must be off."

Resigned, Owen favoured Miranda with a bow and made for the entrance to the gallery, holding the candelabrum aloft so that they might see their way.

Before parting from his lordship, Miranda paused to say, "Good night. And do not despair on account of your engagement. Remember that you do have friends, very devoted friends, of whom I shall forever count myself as one."

On this sentiment, the earl raised her hand to his lips. "I don't deserve such kindness," he murmured.

Owen blushed. He saw the young lady gazing at the earl as though she were daft, and he said angrily, "We must go, Miss Crowther-Biggs."

Ignoring him, the young lady continued, "Oh, you must not say you are undeserving, my lord. It is not your fault you cannot offer for me. And who knows? Perhaps your mama may be brought to change her mind."

Owen said between his teeth, "If you do not come with me at once, miss, then you will have to find your way back in the dark alone."

On this, the earl persuaded Miranda to be led away by his friend. Then he found the door to the terrace. Outside, he breathed in the fragrance of roses in full bloom. He strolled down the wide steps to the wisteria garden, the first in a series of walled gardens for which Lever Combe was renowned. There he found a marble bench a little sheltered from the moonlight by a hedge. Sitting on the bench was a lady, cloaked, hooded, and waiting anxiously.

"What kept you so late?" Cora St. John demanded. "I nearly fell into fidgets thinking you would not come."

Lord Roderick put a fine leg on the bench and leant towards her. "My dear, have I ever failed to keep a rendezvous? Why do you fidget when you know you can rely upon me?"

"What is the use of love if it does not make one fidgety? Fidgets render life interesting. Without fidgets I should be deadly dull."

"Dear Cora, if it makes you happy to fidget, then by all means, be happy."

"Do not quiz me. You are horrible."

"I've never denied it." He lifted her chin so that she looked into his eyes. The he removed the hood of her cloak so that her hair shone in the moonlight. Her lovely face was tight with tension.

Clutching at his hands, she said, "Roddy, why did you wish to meet me tonight? I have not had an easy moment since I received your note."

"I asked you to meet me because I have something to tell you—no, to ask you."

With a smile, she glanced up at him. "I shall grant you anything. You know that."

"Then do not marry Turcott. He is not fit to be a husband; he is a brute."

Her face fell with disappointment. Irritably, she said, "I am weary of widowhood. Turcott has offered for me. No one else has." Here she levelled a significant look at him.

"Cora, you know you ought to break with him. The man is known to be rough and rude. He may have a gentleman's name, but he is not a gentleman."

"It is too late. I have signed agreements. He has power over every farthing that St. John left to me."

"Do not concern yourself about the money, Cora. I will take care of that."

She smiled bitterly. "You will frank my expenses? How very charming. And do you also mean me to live with you as your mistress?"

Amiably, he replied, "I don't mean anything of the kind."

Disappointed again, she stood up. "I don't understand you. You wish me to jilt a man who desires to be my husband. You wish to pay for the jilting. But you will give me neither your name nor your protection. It will not do, Roddy."

"It would not be protection if I were to allow you to come to me. It would be seduction. At least, so the world would say. You would be a scandal everywhere."

"What of it? It might be interesting to be a scandal."

Here his lordship flicked an invisible speck from his boot and removed his leg from the bench. "It would interest you for a while, until the novelty wore off. Then it would be not only dull but lonely, for your acquaintance would cut you."

"I should not care, as long as we were together."

Patiently, he said, "I am not in the market for a mistress."

"Then marry me."

As though he was weary of repeating it, he answered, "I am already engaged to be married. I have told you before."

"Yes, but I don't understand why you do not cry off. How can your mother possibly hold so much

power over you? Your father is dead. You bear his title. What can your mother have to say to anything?''

After a pause, during which he cleared his throat,
he replied, ''It is all set forth in the terms of my father's will. He controls my choice of bride from the
grave, as it were, and my mother, who never went
against him in his lifetime, now refuses to deviate from
his stated wish. But why do I waste time explaining all
this? What is needed is for you to tell Turcott as soon
as possible that you have changed your mind.''

''But I have not changed my mind. I wish to be
married. Widowhood is a great bore. One is always
having to depend on fools and other women's husbands to squire one about.''

''Cora, I am too fond of you to see you ruined forever.'' He spoke with quiet gravity. ''And he *will* ruin
you; you know what he is, though you pretend not
to.''

''I only wish you loved me a little,'' she complained.

At first he considered her seriously. Then he
laughed. ''Ah, you are not going to be vulgar, are
you? You know I regard love as a sentiment best suited
to spaniels and writers of novels. Please,'' he said with
a look she could not resist, ''do not spoil this magnificent summer evening with talk of love.''

LORD RODERICK WALKED swiftly along the gallery,
but before he reached his chamber, he was intercepted by Mrs. Crowther-Biggs, mother of the fair
Miranda. She carried a candelabrum that cast dancing shadows on the walls as she approached. ''Well,
there you are!'' she said accusingly when she reached
him.

"I cannot deny it," he said with a bow. "Here I am."

"This is a fine night's work, I must say. You are a devil, Roddy, a very devil. You are deceiving me with that St. John woman, and you have been avoiding me at every turn."

Sorrowfully, he said, "I sense that you are unhappy with me. Perhaps some sleep will cheer you. And so, good night."

She prevented his departure, saying, "I sent a message to you by way of Mr. Hunt, an angry message, and you ignored it."

"Did he not tell you that he could not find me?"

"Oh, yes, he told me, but I did not believe him. I know you too well to believe such a ruse. You were with a female. I can smell her fragrance on your coat."

He smiled and wagged a playful finger at her. "Livia, you are jealous. How very delightful. Really, I am touched."

"You are no such thing. You are a snake. You are worse than my husband, who is also a snake. Why, you haven't had a moment to spare for me these two days, and tonight you lied to avoid meeting me. This is shabby treatment indeed."

"You wound me, my dear. I have been trying to spare you, but since you will not let me, I shall have to tell you the truth: I was with your daughter tonight."

Even in the dim light he could see the lady go white. "Miranda?"

"She waylaid me. I could not shake her off. And you would not have wanted Mr. Hunt to deliver your message to me in her presence, now would you?"

Swallowing hard, she said, "Of course not. But what was she doing with you?"

"Endeavouring to seduce me."

"She is hardly more than seventeen while you are well past thirty. Do you expect me to believe that she could seduce you?"

"Ah, Livia, the young ones are the worst. They are the most heedless, the most remorseless flirts. Give me the mothers over the daughters any day." Here he gallantly kissed her hand.

This compliment worked its charm, so that she could not help but smile in gratification. "I suppose youth must appear callow to a man of your sensibilities."

"Exactly so."

"But what did you do? You sent her away, I hope."

"Naturally. I told her about my engagement, and she was most sympathetic. She could not stay after that."

Here the lady fanned her white bosom. "Ah, Roddy, I do not understand that engagement of yours. How can you still be engaged? You have not visited Canterbury in ages and ages. You would think the creature would jilt you after such abominable neglect."

"I have no hope that she will jilt me."

She came very near to him and ran a finger along the lapel of his coat. "She would jilt you if you kicked up such a scandal that there was no marrying you at all."

Smiling, he said, "You are thinking something very wicked, I see."

She shrugged. "If you were to go off with a married woman and take up residence in some congenial climate—Switzerland perhaps—then your Canterbury miss would cry off soon enough."

"And your husband would divorce you," he added.

"Nonsense. He would not object to my absence. It is what he cherishes most in me."

The earl kissed her nose. "Running off together would be an excellent strategy, except for one small point. The scandal would leave my mother desolate. Now I put it to you, Livia, you are a mother. How would you feel if it were your child who garnered the scorn of the world and threw away a fortune and an estate all for love?"

Mrs. Crowther-Biggs stepped back, a look of horror suffusing her face. "How do you think I should feel? Such a catastrophe would leave me quite low for days."

"That is what I suspected. You are the most dashing female I ever met, my dear, but as a mother, you are a she-wolf looking out for her cub. I'm afraid my mother is no different."

She sighed. "Oh, Roddy, we mothers do feel things so deeply. It is a curse. I daresay, if I felt less, I might amuse myself more."

Taking both her hands, he pressed them to his breast. "You are magnificent. And now you had better go, lest someone issue from one of these bedrooms and spy us together." Holding her at arm's length, he slowly drew back. Then, blowing her a kiss, he made for his bedchamber, which he contrived to attain without coming upon a single female lying in wait.

THE CUSHIONED CHAIR in the dressing room was occupied by Mr. Owen Hunt, who sipped a glass of brandy and said, "Shall I send for your valet?"

His lordship removed his coat and threw it over a chair. Yawning, he declared, "I am tired, my friend. I shall dispense with the valet tonight, and if you are come to lecture me, be a good fellow, will you, and save it until morning."

"Roderick, I am obliged to tell you, I do not like your toying with such a young girl as Miss Miranda Crowther-Biggs. I thought you had some scruples."

He yawned. "I have no scruples whatsoever; nor have I the least interest in Miss Crowther-Biggs. She is the silliest, most simpering puss I have met in my life."

Offended, Owen retorted hotly, "She happens to be a most charming young lady. She is only very innocent, that is all."

His lordship untied his cravat. "Innocent! You say that because you are such an innocent yourself. Really, Owen, you are *too* innocent. You ought to allow me to introduce you to some of my delightful female acquaintance. Any one of them would be glad to amuse you, purely as a favour to me, you understand."

"What you call amusement alarms my nerves," Mr. Hunt replied primly. "Tonight's nonsense is a prime example. Mrs. Crowther-Biggs sent me to you with a message that you must come at once. She was mad as a hornet and poised to sting—to sting *me* if she could not find you. I recollected your saying that you meant to go out to the garden and so I followed you to the conservatory. And what do I find? That you already had a rendezvous there, and with Miss Crowther-Biggs of all people! Why, I nearly blurted out the message in front of her. She would have perished with mortification to hear such a message from her mother."

"You need not worry, Owen. I have seen Mrs. Crowther-Biggs."

"I suppose there is the devil to pay."

"Don't be absurd. Why should there be?"

"Why? You ask why? Does it not occur to you that one of your females may talk with one of your other females and all your intrigues will explode?"

"As a matter of fact, it does not."

"I do not understand how you can be so insouciant."

"Why should I fret, Owen? You fret so energetically on my behalf. My fretting would only be redundant. I find the arrangement vastly pleasing—you see to the fretting while I see to the ladies."

"You joke while I anticipate an early grave," Owen mourned.

Roderick smiled fondly. "I have used you ill, and I am very sorry for it. You are too good a friend, better than I deserve. You ought to cut me, you know."

"I shall do no such thing. If I do not watch out for you, who will be there to collect what is left of you after the débâcle comes? I picked up the various scattered pieces of you at Oxford and on the battlefield. It is what I shall continue to do while it is necessary."

"I wish you were not so loyal to a blackguard."

"You are not a blackguard. You are a fool. Why else would you make love to every female in England?"

"Do not forget Scotland. I hunt every season in Scotland."

"Why do you do it, Roderick? Purely for the sport?"

Having thrown his cravat over the chair, his lordship sighed restlessly. "I suppose there is a certain sporting element. But I am also very much in earnest. These women—young and old, beautiful and plain,

rich and poor—are the saving of me. They are exactly
like me, moved by a profound wish to alleviate their
ennui with a little adventure. I accommodate them by
bringing an element of danger into their lives. In their
turn, they bring a little softness into mine. It is a fair
bargain. They have never complained; nor do I complain. I am content."

"Oh, yes! I can see very well how content you are,
as content as the sheep when the storms sweep down
from the sea. You are restless and dissatisfied. I wish
you would marry. At least then I should not have to
live in dread of your getting your head shot off by
some thwarted female or her jealous husband. At least
then you would be settled."

"I would be settled," said his lordship amiably as
he removed his shirt, "but I should not be half so well
entertained."

"What you are doing is dangerous. One of these
ladies may fall in love with you. No doubt she will
want to marry you, and then you will be in a fix."

"Not in the least. Have you forgotten my Canterbury tale?"

"How can I forget it? There is not a day that I do
not fear you will be caught in the lie."

"Such a calamity might prove interesting, don't you
agree?"

"I most certainly do not agree. And what do you
intend to do when your mother gets wind of this tale
of yours?"

"I shall be in a pickle. My only recourse will be to
enter a monastery, take a vow of chastity, and live on
hard bread and treacle. It sounds rather a pleasant life,
I think."

"The women would not allow it. They would storm the place."

Roderick laughed. He was prevented from pursuing this interesting line of conversation, however, by a light scratching at the door. To Owen's despair, a musical female voice enquired through the oak, "Are you awake, my lord? Might I have a word?"

CHAPTER THREE

The Scheme

SOME DAYS AFTER their visit to the cathedral, Lucy and Lady Philpott entered the north saloon at Queenscroft to find Lady Roderick in a pet. She walked up and down the room, almost wearing a path in the flowered carpet. So absorbed was she that she did not see the ladies enter, and it took many *ahems* on the part of Lady Philpott to win her hostess's attention.

Lady Roderick threw a stricken look at her friends, saying, "He has done it again."

Lady Philpott drew near, while Lucy discreetly sat at a little distance.

"Who has done what?" asked Lady Philpott.

"Roderick. My son. The joy of my life, and the blight of it, as well."

Lady Philpott said, "Lord Roderick, you say? I believe he is unmarried. Is that not so?"

The countess stared ahead. "Unmarried? He is the most unmarried man in all of Britain!"

At this assurance, Lady Philpott directed a significant look at Lucy. "Well, at least he will not go running off to war again. His duty is to stay at home, marry and produce an heir, especially now that he has inherited his father's title."

"Do not speak of his father!" cried Lady Roderick. "He is just *like* his father!"

Seeing the lady so distraught, Lucy approached and quietly assisted her to the sofa. She induced her to sit, while Lady Philpott sat beside her and replied agreeably, "Of course he is like his father, and why shouldn't he be? The earl was an indulgent, sweet-tempered husband and very rich."

Lady Roderick seized her friend's hand and said urgently, "Yes, but that was after we were married. Before that, he was a perfect rake."

"Why, yes, I recollect hearing something of his reputation. I believe it was said he rivalled Don Juan in the number of his conquests. Tell me, was it true?"

"It was worse, much worse."

"Gracious me," said Lady Philpott, fanning herself. "I had no idea he was such an interesting fellow. But how did you contrive to change him after your marriage?"

"I did not change him. He apparently had had enough of the rake's life and wished to settle. Therefore, settle he did."

"Indeed, he did settle," Lady Philpott confided to Lucy, who stood by Lady Roderick in case some wine should be required. "He grew so attached to his home that he was rarely seen in London."

Kneeling beside Lady Roderick, Lucy asked quietly, "Would you feel easier if I left you alone? Perhaps you would like to discuss the matter with Lady Philpott in private."

"No!" exclaimed the lady. "Do not leave me, for if there is anyone who will understand what heartbreak a scoundrel can wreak, it is you, Miss Bledsoe."

At this reference, Lucy felt her cheeks grow warm.

"My son," said Lady Roderick, "is exactly as Lady Philpott has described Sir Vale Saunders. He is a perfect scoundrel, and if you do not believe me, then read this." On this, she handed Lucy a letter. "Go ahead," she said hoarsely, "read it."

"Do read it aloud," said Lady Philpott. "Nothing is so pleasant as being read to."

Unfolding the paper, Lucy read as follows:

"To Lady Fanny Roderick, Countess of Silverthorne:

I beg you will forgive my taking the liberty of addressing you on a matter of the greatest intimacy, but I cannot remain silent a moment longer. It is true I am a stranger to you, but I am very well acquainted with his lordship, your son, and hold him in the highest possible esteem. My purpose in writing is to plead with you to release him from your thrall and that of the young lady in Canterbury to whom he is engaged. He has confided to me that he does not love the lady. It is immoral, I think, to press him to marry where he does not love. If my mama endeavoured to coerce me in such a manner, I should be forced to run away. I should run to Italy, for I have heard many delightful tales of that warm clime. Or I should go to Greece. The West Indies are said to be exotic, and I have always been curious to see the grandeur of Canada, as well. In any case, I should not do as your son so devotedly and faithfully does, namely, continue to honour the irrational wishes of a beloved parent. Surely if you regarded your duty to your son one-tenth as

much as he regards his duty to you, you would
release him from his promise to marry and en-
able him to choose freely. If that choice should be
me, I should count myself the most fortunate female alive. Forgive me for leaving this unsigned,
as Mama would fly out at me if she ever found
out I had written to you.

> I am, etc.,
> A Lady"

"What a remarkable, letter," said Lady Philpott.
Lucy refolded the paper before returning it.

"What do you think of such a letter?" Lady Roderick asked her. "You are a sensible and feeling young
lady. I wish to know your opinion of such a letter and
of such a son."

Gazing into the distressed woman's face, Lucy replied, "Have you considered the likelihood that this
is a prank, a very ill-mannered, silly prank, to be sure,
but not to be taken seriously?"

"Oh, if only it were a prank. But I have other letters of the same kind, and not just from daughters, but
from mothers, and even grandmothers, pleading with
me to release my son from his promise to marry a girl
in Canterbury."

As gently as she could, Lucy said, "Then perhaps
there is some justice in what the letter writer says. Her
impudence, her inelegance of expression, her foolish-
ness notwithstanding, if your son keeps to his engagement only because you insist upon it, then you must
release him."

Here Lady Roderick abruptly rose, causing Lucy
and Lady Philpott to rise also. "But he is not en-

gaged! There is no young lady in Canterbury. It is all invention!''

"I do not understand," cried Lady Philpott. "Why should your son invent such a tale?"

The countess looked at Lucy. "I wonder if Miss Bledsoe can guess," she said. "I wonder if after the ill fortune she met with at Bath, she can deduce the reason for my son's arrant falsehood."

Lucy saw the manner in which Lady Roderick looked at her, as though they shared a hideous fate, that of being attached to a scoundrel, and the recognition pained her. She was forced to seek out a chair and take a moment to collect herself. She was forced to acknowledge that all the churches and ruins of Kent had not succeeded in quelling her feelings in regard to scoundrels. So powerful was the recognition that she was constrained to catch her breath. All too well did she guess the gentleman's reason for lying.

"I believe," Lucy said unevenly to Lady Philpott, "that Lord Roderick has invented the tale in order to have a convincing reason why he cannot marry. If he has such a reason, then he is at liberty to flirt with all the ladies he meets without having to offer for any of them. It is most convenient."

It took some time before Lady Philpott comprehended the enormity of his lordship's scheme. When she did, she began to smile in admiration. "Why, he is the very devil of a rogue, isn't he?" she remarked.

"He is in every way horrid," said Lady Roderick. "He makes his own poor mother out to be a harpy. My reputation throughout the kingdom will soon be a shambles."

Lady Philpott clucked, shaking her head, still smiling. "What a wicked, wicked thing for him to do. Tell me, is he very handsome?"

Weakly, Lady Roderick gestured vaguely in the direction of the fireplace. "His miniature is over there," she said.

Lady Philpott went in search of it. She found a small table arranged with a dozen or so miniatures. Finding the one with the handsomest likeness, she brought it to her friend. "Is this your son?" she asked hopefully.

Glaring at the portrait, Lady Roderick replied, "It is."

Thereupon, Lady Philpott brought the miniature to Lucy. "What do you think of that, my dear girl?" she said, placing it in her hand.

Lucy glanced briefly at the handsome face, then glanced away. She had seen such faces before, graced with a well-formed brow and a pair of expressive dark eyes. His lip curled on one side, producing an arrogant smile, the smile of a man who saw through a woman, who sought out the weakness in her heart. When he had located the spot where she was most likely to be vulnerable, he pounced, like a lion upon a hart. Without even knowing the Earl of Silverthorne, she felt she knew him. Without even knowing him, she despised him.

"What do you think?" asked Lady Philpott, repeating the question.

"He is well enough," said Lucy in a tranquil voice, but inside she brimmed with emotion. Unable to remain seated, she stood and walked the length of the room. Then, looking down, she saw that she still held the miniature. The fine face was framed by dark curls.

The brown eyes gazed at her starkly. There was peril in their light.

"What am I going to do?" Lady Roderick implored. "Can I leave such lies unanswered? Am I to remain silent while the world censures me for coercing my son into a loveless match?"

"You might give him a scold," said Lady Philpott. "If he knew you did not like the story, I daresay he would give it up."

"You do not know the worst of it. Whenever he comes to me and I complain to him, he charms me out of countenance, so that I do not know what I am saying and forget to tell him that I am angry. The last time he came to visit, I vow, he made me weep with laughter, though I was in a perfect rage over his abominable conduct. I cannot think when he is by. No wonder the ladies are impelled to write to me. They are as foolish as I am!"

Here Lady Philpott said, "He sounds a very charming gentleman. I daresay Lucy and I should like to meet him. Do you by any chance expect him at Queenscroft any time soon?"

The countess went to Lucy and took her hands. "My dear, I know that you must be sensible of my difficulty. Your intimate knowledge of the ways of a scoundrel must make you pity me."

"Indeed it does," said Lucy warmly, "and I pity all the ladies who are ensnared by his lordship's lies. I think it is too bad that such a lie is permitted to go unanswered. I think it ought to be answered and in a way that will teach the gentleman a sound lesson."

Her listeners were curious to hear what way that might be.

"Lady Roderick," Lucy said, reining in her emotion, "where did you say your son was staying at present?"

"At Lever Combe, the house of Lord and Lady Knatchbull."

"I think that his lordship's betrothed ought to pay a visit to Lever Combe."

"But I've told you, there is no betrothed. It is pure tale-spinning on my son's part."

Lucy smiled softly. "There is no betrothed now, but perhaps there might be. We might find a young lady to impersonate her. She would arrive at Lord and Lady Knatchbull's house and play the part. His lies would soon come crashing down about his ears, and his ladies would have nothing more to do with him."

The countess clapped her hands in raptures, but Lady Philpott gaped in astonishment. "Miss Bledsoe!" she exclaimed. "I had no notion you were capable of such plotting. Lord Roderick is rich, titled and handsome; such men have the right to amuse themselves a little, you know. It is not as though they were bound by the same rules of conduct as ordinary men."

Lucy was too engrossed to hear. "Where shall we find such a young woman? That is the question," she said. Having originated the scheme, she now warmed to it. The idea of giving his lordship his comeuppance was singularly gratifying to her, especially as she had let Sir Vale leave without treating him to the reproofs he deserved.

"Why could *you* not do it?" enquired Lady Roderick.

"Me?" cried Lucy, aghast. "Impossible. I am no actress."

"But it would require very little in the way of acting," Lady Roderick urged.

"I should be frightened of discovery." She shivered at the thought.

"But the threat of discovery is no obstacle. Let Roderick learn in good time that we have played him a trick. It will serve him right."

Lucy tried to imagine herself playing the role and ended by shaking her head. "I don't think I could pull it off."

"Nonsense. You underrate yourself. Besides, you would not have to go alone. Lady Philpott would accompany you to Lever Combe." Turning to her friend, Lady Roderick asked, "Will you not go with her, Mathilde?"

Lady Philpott folded her arms and considered the situation. It occurred to her that if Lucy did go to Lever Combe, she might meet one or two eligible gentlemen, which she had nary a chance of doing if she stayed at Queenscroft. It also occurred to her that one of the eligible gentleman Lucy would meet would be no less a personage than Lord Roderick, Earl of Silverthorne, who had twelve thousand a year, lands in Kent and Scotland, and a mother with a famous collection of emeralds. It did not trouble Lady Philpott that Lucy would go to Lever Combe on an errand of revenge. She had no doubt that the young lady would take one look at the roguish gentleman, fall head over ears in love with him and forget revenge. Every women loved a rogue in her heart of hearts, Lady Philpott believed, and would much rather catch a title than teach a lesson. Therefore, she said, "I agree with Lady Roderick. I think we ought to go to Lever Combe at once."

Lucy now regretted her inspiration. It was one thing to advise others how to deal with their difficulties, but quite another to become embroiled in the solution. "I do not think we need embark on such a scheme after all," she said hastily. "You may write your son a letter, Lady Roderick. You may explain your feelings in regard to his lie, and I am certain he will do what he may to oblige you."

"He may oblige me," said the exasperated mother, "but he will not have learned his lesson. He will concoct another scheme, and I do not know what I shall do if he implicates me again. I am the mildest creature in all the world, but will not have my good name muddied, not even by my son—especially not by my son. I have spoilt him. That is why he behaves as he does. You may help me unspoil him, if only you will."

"I have no wish to spend any more time in the company of scoundrels than I already have," Lucy said in a quiet voice that concealed but did not quell her feelings. "I cannot do it."

"If you cannot," said Lady Roderick dejectedly, "then no one can. Any other young lady would be sure to fall in love with Roderick and forget all about teaching him a lesson. But you, having so lately fortified yourself against such men, would be proof against his wiles."

Lucy was not as certain as her ladyship that she would be strong in the face of Lord Roderick's attractions. Judging by the miniature she held in her hand, those attractions were compelling. Moreover, just days ago she had once again succumbed to Sir Vale's charms. Even now, she felt the stirrings of an unwilling attachment to him. She had summoned the strength to repulse his advances, but she continued to

think of him. It did not seem to her that she had sufficiently recovered her heart to contend with another
such gentleman.

On the other hand, she desired more than anything
to leave Canterbury, where the incessant gossip and
compassionate stares of the townsfolk kept her from
going about as she would have liked. Furthermore, she
might take a visit to Lever Combe as an opportunity
to test herself. In teaching Lord Roderick a lesson, she
might strengthen her own character, reaffirm her resolve, and prove to herself that even a broken-hearted
Lucy Bledsoe might withstand the charms of a scoundrel.

"Well, I suppose I might put in an appearance for
an evening," Lucy said carefully.

"An evening is nothing!" cried Lady Philpott, who
did not see how a match could be made up between
Lucy and the earl if she was only to show herself for a
few hours. "In this age of dissipation, gentleman
cannot be taught lessons in anything less than a
month."

Horrified, Lucy repeated, "A month! I could not
possibly maintain such a pretense for so long. Indeed, I should be fortunate to keep my countenance
for a fortnight."

"Then a fortnight it is!" Lady Philpott declared
triumphantly. "A month is much to be preferred, but
if we must make do with two weeks, I suppose I must
say nothing and resign myself to your will." Here her
ladyship sighed heavily and endeavoured to look resigned, but a sparkle of glee played in her eyes, for to
have won a promise of two weeks from the future
Countess of Silverthorne was as much of a victory in
her eyes as anything General Wellington could boast.

LADY KNATCHBULL GAZED from the window in despair. Her guests, who had been forced to stay indoors for three days, were growing restless and snappish, and there was no sign in the grey sky that the rain ever intended to stop.

With Lord Knatchbull leading the way, the gentlemen joined the ladies in the drawing room. There Lord Roderick persuaded Miss Crowther-Biggs to relieve the tedium by sitting down to the pianoforte and favouring them with "Wellington's March." Her mother stood nearby, turning the girl's pages, while his lordship threw meaningful glances at each of them in turn.

Her ladyship, noticing that Cora St. John yawned and fussed with the fringe of her gown, engaged her in conversation, and although it was early, Lord Knatchbull induced Owen Hunt and the other guests to make up a card table. It promised to be a dull, tiresome evening such as can only be enjoyed in the country, when the footman entered bearing a note on a salver. The lady of the house opened the note to read:

My dear Letitia,
   This introduces to your acquaintance Miss Lucy Bledsoe, who is engaged to my son Lord Roderick, and her companion, Lady Philpott. I know I may rely on your hospitality to welcome the young lady. She is shy and would not have dared to impose on your goodness had I not persuaded her that you are the best creature in the world and that she has been separated far too long from the man who is the centre of all her affections and hopes.

I am ever your devoted,
Fanny Roderick

Lady Knatchbull bolted from her chair, then read the note again. Lord Roderick engaged? Why, he had been flirting with two generations of Crowther-Biggs for the past weeks. Moreover, his conduct had given rise to some speculation that he contemplated an elopement with Mrs. St. John. She herself had fallen half in love with the man. How was it possible that he had been engaged all this time and that his lady love had now arrived on her doorstep? She was all amazement. However, she was too curious not to go and see the young person for herself.

Lucy and Lady Philpott stood in the great hall before the enormous fireplace. They allowed the servants to take their wet cloaks as Lady Knatchbull came forward to greet them. The moment she saw her hostess, Lucy's heart nearly failed her, but a poke in the ribs from Lady Philpott kept her from losing courage.

"You are a very elegant young lady," said her ladyship to Lucy as she took in her pale green gauze dress, cut low at the neck and trimmed with an embroidered ribbon. She then turned to Lady Philpott, whom she inspected with somewhat less approval, for she had no opinion of boldly coloured hat feathers which bounced up and down in the air, and she certainly had no opinion of the women who wore such frippery.

"You are kind to indulge us," said Lady Philpott with unction. "And if you will allow me, I shall go and inform his lordship who has arrived. He has had no warning of our coming and will be vastly surprised."

"Certainly," said Lady Knatchbull. "I shall have the servant conduct you."

On that, Lady Philpott swept after the footman. At the door to the drawing room, she scanned the room. The original of the miniature she had seen in Lady Roderick's sitting room stood by the pianoforte. He looked handsomer than his likeness, for his tall figure, dressed sumptuously in a smoky blue coat and buff-coloured breeches, added to the impression he gave of classic good looks. She smacked her lips in anticipation of the challenge before her, then crowed in a voice loud enough to cause everyone in the room to turn and look at her, "My dear Lord Roderick, I bring you a surprise."

He glanced up from a page of music he was reading and favoured the lady with an enchanting, if puzzled, smile. "I beg your pardon. Are we acquainted?"

Lady Philpott approached him as every eye on the room followed her. "I am Lady Philpott, of whom you never heard in your life. I am just come from Canterbury."

"A quaint town, Canterbury," said his lordship pleasantly. "I trust you enjoyed your stay."

"It bored me to extinction. Nevertheless, I bring you a surprise from there."

He laughed.

"Are you not perishing to see the surprise?" she demanded.

Lord Roderick looked at Owen Hunt. Owen replied to that look with an innocent shrug. He knew nothing of any surprise, and so his shrug informed the earl.

"Is it my birthday already?" his lordship asked. "Surely I have just had a birthday and cannot be older again so soon."

Lady Philpott replied gaily, "You know very well it is not your birthday, my lord."

"Well, I suppose I shall have to have a look at this surprise, whatever it is. A surprise must always be welcome."

"Especially such one as this!" Glancing around, Lady Philpott saw Lucy in the doorway next to Lady Knatchbull. With a sweeping gesture in their direction she said, "Lord Roderick, I present to you...your betrothed."

His lordship blinked. As he watched the elegant young woman glide toward him, he could find nothing to say. She drew near, making him potently aware of a glow of blue eyes, wisps of honey-coloured curls, a slender, graceful form and a neck of unsurpassed delectability. He did not trouble to disguise his admiration, but took her hand when she extended it to him and raised it to his lips.

"Roderick, my dear," Lucy intoned in a breathy voice. "How do you do?"

"I hardly know," he said, suspended between amusement and amazement.

Because he held tightly to her hand, she rapped him on the shoulder with her fan. "You naughty, naughty man," she said.

Lady Philpott addressed the fascinated onlookers then, saying, "They have been engaged these hundred years at least, but have not seen each other since, well, I hardly know when."

"Roddy, when was the last time we saw each other?" Lucy asked him with a glittering smile.

"It was in a dream," he said warmly, "a haunting dream."

Tossing her head, Lucy laughed and confided to the company, "He is such a flirt. If we had not plighted our troth, I should not trust him out of my sight."

At this sally, Miranda Crowther-Biggs let forth a wrenching sob. She fell forward onto the keys of the pianoforte, causing everyone to wince at the cacophonous result, and begged her mama to take her away. Owen Hunt went to her instantly to see whether he might be of assistance.

Lucy, too, went to the young lady, peered down at her and said, "Oh, you are unwell. Did I interrupt your playing?"

Miranda raised a tear-streaked face and said, "With all my heart, I hate you!"

Lucy smiled, taking confidence from this testimony to the effectiveness of her performance. Owen and Mrs. Crowther-Biggs helped Miranda to her feet. Holding the girl's shoulders as she wept, the mother shot a fiery glance at Lord Roderick, snapping, "How dare you permit that female to come here? It will not go well with you if I find you have sent for her."

Lucy, who found the mother's threat as gratifying as the daughter's hatred, remembered to affix a sorrowful expression to her face as the ladies went out. Then, addressing Lady Knatchbull, she said, "Perhaps the young lady fears that I might rival her skill at the pianoforte. You must put her mind at rest at once. My teachers could not wring a single melody from these poor hands." Here she extended her graceful hands so that they nearly reached to Owen Hunt, who looked at her as though she were the Angel of Death come to pay a call. After a moment of regarding the gentleman, she said to him, "I vow, sir, why do you stare at me in such a manner? Has my lace slipped?"

Owen rasped, "Who the deuce are you?"

"Why, I am Lucy Bledsoe of Canterbury, and I am promised to that gentleman there. And who might you be?"

Lord Roderick came forward and said amiably, "Permit me, my dear, to present you to my good friend Owen Hunt, of whom you have heard me speak so often. Owen, say 'how do you do' to the lady who is soon to be my *cara sposa*."

Confused, Lucy met Lord Roderick's smiling eyes. She found herself unnerved by his unflagging good manners. She had not anticipated his maintaining such equanimity and had fully expected him to fly into a temper at her appearance. But he neither denied her nor endeavoured to expose her. All he did was favour her with an amused expression and the observation, "Owen will, I know, be delighted to meet you at last, my dear Miss Bledsoe. He has long been wishing I would marry."

Owen burst into a fit of coughing and a glass of wine was quickly brought for his relief.

Meanwhile, Cora St. John brushed past Lady Philpott and stood before Lucy. Appraising her fiercely, she declared, "You are a fraud!"

Frightened by the words as well as the wildness with which they were spoken, Lucy put her hand to her breast and stepped back. Lord Roderick came forward to intercede.

"He does not love you," Cora hissed. "He never will."

"Mrs. St. John," the earl said smoothly, "I have the honour to present Miss Lucy Bledsoe of the Canterbury Bledsoes.'' During the introduction, he managed to place himself between the two ladies so that no harm might come of their encounter.

Mrs. St. John inclined her head coldly towards the new arrival. Lucy murmured something polite, after which they all shifted about, wondering what to do with themselves.

Lucy searched in her mind for something to say. Although she had begun well enough, she was swiftly growing alarmed. Her appearance had certainly put a number of Lady Knatchbull's guests into a pother. The girl at the pianoforte and her mother had displayed a gratifying agitation, while Mrs. St. John had been as resentful and Owen Hunt as shocked as she could have wished. But Lord Roderick had remained unperturbed throughout the entire proceeding. Such unaccountable insouciance left her at a loss.

At last she concluded it was best to decamp, so as to reconnoitre with Lady Philpott. Accordingly, she said to Lady Knatchbull, ''I'm afraid my coming unannounced has been an inconvenience. Lady Philpott and I will return to the inn where we are staying, and we will not impose on your goodness any further.'' She moved to Lady Philpott, slipped her arm through hers and would have led her out the door, when she heard behind her the deep voice of Lord Roderick imploring, ''Oh, Lucy, do not leave me now, after so long and so painful a separation.'' Here he fell to one knee with an arm stretched towards her.

The guests lifted themselves halfway out of their chairs so that they might observe him as he spoke from the floor.

Lucy stopped. Without turning to face him, she said, "And whose fault is our long and painful separation, sir?"

He rose, straightened his shoulders and approached. With a wink at Lady Philpott, he induced that good woman to step aside, enabling him to draw close to Lucy's back. She tensed, feeling his breath on her shoulder as he said, "Whose fault is it? you ask. You know perfectly well it is your fault. You have treated me cruelly."

Stung, she whipped round to face him and saw the guests straining their ears to hear what might come next. Their stares forced her to collect herself. "If I have treated you cruelly," she answered, shaken, "it is because you have dealt treacherously with me."

"If I have dealt treacherously with you," he said pleasantly, "it is because you have treated me cruelly."

Seeing that this sort of exchange could go back and forth all night, Lucy said, "It is late. Lady Philpott and I must bid you good-night now."

He seized her hand and pressed it between both of his. The gentlemen in the room nodded at this bold gesture, the ladies fanned their necks.

"Do not go," he said. "Not until we have forgiven each other."

"I have done nothing to be forgiven for!" Lucy cried. "Let go of my hand."

"Lady Knatchbull," said the earl, as though powerful feeling had robbed him of the sense to know that he caressed a woman's hand, "could you find it in your heart to ask Miss Bledsoe and her charming companion to stay the night? Surely you will not permit my beloved to run away just when she is come to me at last."

Her ladyship, who had not provided her guests with so much entertainment in days, was well disposed to proffer an invitation; so well disposed, in fact, that she invited the ladies to stay the week.

"We should be delighted to stay *two* weeks," put in Lady Philpott.

"I must not impose on your hospitality, Lady Knatchbull," Lucy said nervously. Now that she had performed her masquerade, she was anxious to put some distance between herself and the earl, at least long enough to consider her next step.

Abruptly, Lord Roderick let go of Lucy's slender hand and took Lady Philpott's plump, beringed one. Her ladyship watched with approval as he raised it to his lips. "Dear Lady Philpott," he intoned, "will you not take pity on me?"

"Of course, you poor man," Lady Philpott cooed.

"And will you not persuade my cruel tormentor to accept Lady Knatchbull's invitation?"

"If by 'cruel tormentor' you mean Lucy, I certainly shall persuade her."

"And will you not be the means of reconciling us, so that we may be happy all the rest of our days?"

Lady Philpott glanced from his lordship's dark, mischievous eyes to Lucy's blue ones and, sensing that victory was within her grasp, gave her answer.

CHAPTER FOUR

Tête-à-tête

MORNING WOKE Lord Roderick betimes, and when he had ascertained that he was in his own bed, he called for his valet to dress him. There was no time to lose if he was going to glean information from this unexpected Miss Lucy Bledsoe. He anticipated their next meeting with pleasure, for the lady had surprised him, a feat which no female had accomplished since he was out of leading strings. In the eventful years since then, he had wooed, won and wearied of countless females, but not one of them had been permitted to call herself his betrothed—a title he had no intention of bestowing upon any female creature until he was absolutely driven to it.

What was it about Miss Bledsoe that surprised him? It was not merely her pose. Nor was it the elegance of her walk—though it was difficult to take one's eyes from her when she walked. Elegance in the female sex did not surprise him any more than pretense did. What did surprise him was to find such elegance in an imposter.

He recollected now the gentleness of her blue eyes, the delicacy of her shoulders, the pale green gauze of the gown that clung to her form and the earnest tone with which she had told him that she had nothing to be forgiven for. Miss Lucy Bledsoe was undoubtedly the most interesting female he had met in many a year.

She amused him, too. Not only had she scolded him roundly for being a flirt, but she had addressed Owen Hunt and the others in an airy manner which hinted that she knew a good deal about him. Nothing was so flattering as to be known by a stranger. Moreover, the intelligence behind her pretense was unmistakable. It was a quality the earl had sought in a woman since he was a young man full of illusions, and in seeing Miss Bledsoe that day, he meant to spar with her again, to assure himself that his original impression had been correct.

In the breakfast parlour sat the wife and daughter of Mr. Crowther-Biggs, along with Cora St. John. Mrs. Crowther-Biggs informed the earl with asperity that the other gentlemen had breakfasted early and were preparing to walk out to look over some traps set by poachers. Each of the ladies did her best to punish his lordship with a cold air and lack of attention. Seeing their pique, he smiled, thinking that an engagement was not a bad thing if it purchased him respite from flirtation. Dalliance was all very well, but it wore out a fellow, rendered him insensible to feminine arts and gave him the insatiable longing for something fresh.

When Lady Philpott entered the breakfast parlour, his lordship smiled expectantly, but Miss Bledsoe did not follow. He soon learned that she had had chocolate brought to her bedchamber, whence she did not intend to stir for the remainder of the day.

"She says she is indisposed," said Lady Philpott, "and I cannot persuade her otherwise."

"I shall send a note to her," he replied amiably.

The three ladies glanced up from their kidney and toast to glare at him. Seeing their disapproval, he treated them to a dazzling smile, saying, "You would think me horrid if I did not pay proper attention to my betrothed."

"I think you horrid now," declared Mrs. St. John, throwing down her fork so that it clattered on the plate. In another instant, she rose and stalked from the parlour.

Miss Crowther-Biggs burst into tears and ran from the room. Before her mother followed her, she informed his lordship, "I am well aware you flaunt that female before me merely to mortify my pride. You did not have the face to break with me like a man; therefore, you sent for that creature to save your wicked skin." On that, she bustled out to solace her daughter.

Left alone with Lady Philpott, his lordship tasted a forkful of breakfast, and observed, "Dear me, it appears the ladies are displeased."

"I do believe they are jealous." She, too, attacked her breakfast with relish.

"Ah, you flatter me, madam."

She paused in her chewing. "I never flatter the gentlemen. They are too busy seeing to the business themselves. No, the ladies seem to think Miss Lucy Bledsoe poaches their game."

He folded his arms and sat back to regard her. "What do you suppose could have given them such an idea?"

Lady Philpott returned his roguish look with a scold. "I expect you gave them that idea, my lord. As Miss Bledsoe said last night, you are a naughty, naughty man."

His smile was replaced by a laugh. He poked at a bit of sausage, remarking, "You do not approve of me, I collect."

"You are mistaken, sir. I approve heartily."

Liking the sound of that, he said, "I treasure your approval, madam. I should also treasure a little information. Who and what is this Miss Lucy Bledsoe?"

Although Lady Philpott liked the gentleman's silky manner and thought it would suit Lucy admirably, she was not about to give out any information prematurely. She therefore said, "You know very well she is the young woman from Canterbury whom you are to marry. Who else should she be?"

"By which you mean to say that you will not tell me anything."

"But which I mean to say that I can think of no more charming pair than you and Miss Bledsoe." She pointed her fork at him. "The sooner your engagement culminates in marriage, the happier I shall be."

"My dear lady, I beg you not to speak of marriage. Its only use is to be the means by which respectable folk may earn their bread. As I am fortunate enough to be amazingly rich, I have no need to marry, and certainly no desire to. I do, however, long to see once more this young lady who intends to be my bride." Calling for a writing desk, he penned a short note. When he had blotted the words and folded the paper, he invited her ladyship to wait whilst the servant was sent to deliver it.

A MOMENT LATER Lucy read:

My dear Miss Bledsoe,
    It is my greatest wish to further my acquain-

tance with the enchanting young lady to whom I
find myself betrothed. Will you walk out with me
in the wisteria garden this morning?

Faithfully yours,
Roderick

Lucy refolded the note with a smile. She had re-
solved to keep to her chamber the entire day expressly
to pique his lordship's vanity. At first, she had
planned to reprove the earl when next they met. To
prepare herself, she had rehearsed a number of scolding phrases designed to reason him out of his scoundrel's ways. But the phrases had sounded prosing and
ridiculous. Moreover, it occurred to her that bald
morality was never a very effective means of teaching
anybody anything. Much more effective would be a
refusal to be charmed by him. Let him find that there
was one member of the female species who was impervious to his flattery, one who did not for a moment believe his look of admiration, one who did not
leap at his invitation to walk out. Therefore, taking up
writing materials from the small escritoire in her
chamber, she replied,

My dear Lord Roderick,
    I am indisposed and will not walk today. How
very much it entertains me to see you sign yourself 'Faithfully yours.'

Yours etc.,
L.B.

Lord Roderick showed Lady Philpott the note, detected enough encouragement in the lady's expression
to ascertain that he would have an ally in that quarter

and announced he would join the other gentlemen. He
had a better chance of catching the neighbourhood
game poachers, he said, than of setting eyes on the
reclusive Miss Bledsoe that day.

Lady Philpott lost no time in reporting to Lucy
where the earl had gone. In her turn, Lucy lost no time
in seizing her bonnet and making for the garden,
where she meant to admire the delectable red, yellow
and pink roses she had seen from the window. She
longed to enjoy their fragrance while she could. It was
mid-August already and the time for roses would soon
be at an end. To the roses, therefore, she went.

She was questioning the gardener on some matters
of cultivation, when she turned round to see Lord
Roderick approaching along the path. Spying a door
in the stone wall, she asked the gardener where it led.
He informed her that it opened on a lyme walk which
ended at St. Nicholas Church. Taking the door at
once, she escaped into the cool shadows of the lyme
trees. She walked quickly to the church, inspected its
red jasper walls, its grey, weathered gravestones and its
green wide-armed yew until she was certain that Lord
Roderick had had sufficient time to return to the
house.

She was retracing her steps along the lyme walk,
when suddenly a figure stepped from behind one of
the trees, surprising her. ''Mr. Hunt,'' she said.

He bowed curtly. ''Miss Bledsoe. You will forgive
me if I appear ill-mannered, but I am compelled to ask
whether Miss Bledsoe is indeed your name.''

Liking the young man's serious air, she replied
gently, ''Yes, it is.''

His face took on an expression of such distress that
Lucy was moved to say, ''I am sorry if you do not like

the name. I have always thought it serviceable, though undistinguished."

He shook his head, as if her being called "Lucy Bledsoe" rendered his situation most desperate. "What are you doing here?" he cried. "What do you want from Roderick? If it is money, you may tell me how much and I will see that you get it."

"Money? Does he think I want money?" The idea entertained her hugely.

"You evidently want something. Money seems the most likely object."

She pondered his suggestion. No one had ever mistaken her, the refined Miss Bledsoe, for a blackmailer. She refrained from laughter, however, for her companion was as grave as death. "I am sorry to have distressed you," she said, "but I am curious to know how much his lordship wishes to offer."

Owen gasped, "So it *is* money you are after!"

"That depends on what he thinks I am worth. What is the price of a bride nowadays?"

Oblivious to the laughter in her eyes, Owen was scandalized. "I would not have believed it. From your air, your manner, your elegance, I felt sure you could not be mercenary."

These encomiums made Lucy repent her laughter. Gently, she said, "You are very kind. I truly regret it if my being mercenary distresses you. Everything I say seems to distress you; yet none of it appears to distress his lordship."

Owen sighed heavily. "I know. It is most distressing."

Lucy took a step closer so that she stood in a beam of sunlight filtering through the lyme branches. "Mr. Hunt, let us forget his lordship for the moment and speak of you." In answer to his look of wonder, she said softly, "I do not think it wise for you to be so fretful. You will harm your good health."

Wretchedly, he shook his head. "If I do not fret, who will?"

"You are too young and too kind to repine. My companion, Lady Philpott, always recommends that young people fall in love to forget their troubles. I believe in your case she would certainly recommend such a cure."

He coloured. Something in the lady's kind concern made him confess, "To say the truth, I am a little in love."

"Excellent! You must go and find the lady and see if she will permit you to walk out with her."

Staring off into the distance, he sighed again, this time quite miserably. "She does not know I am alive. You see, she is in love with Lord Roderick."

Lucy's eyes clouded at this news. It did not raise the earl in her esteem to learn that he had engaged the affections of the young lady admired by his friend. "You do not know how sorry I am to hear it," she said.

He eyed her curiously. "Why should you be sorry?"

"Because you are an excellent young man and deserve to be happy. Indeed, I wish you every happiness." Here she gave him a heartening look and marched off towards the garden door.

Owen stared after her, thinking that for a fraud and a cheat, Miss Bledsoe was a female of amazing benevolence.

Poor Mr. Hunt, Lucy thought as she opened the garden door and passed through. He was another reason why his lordship needed a sound lesson. It was not enough that the scoundrel broke women's hearts; he must also be the means of breaking the hearts of good and honest men.

"What are you thinking?" asked a voice.

There before her, backed by a flame-coloured shrub, stood the Earl of Silverthorne. He wore a dark green coat with velvet collar and a tidy white cravat. He raised his hat as he went on to say, "You were so deep in thought that I was curious to know what you were thinking." He smiled. "I dare not hope that your thoughts dwelt on me."

Seeing no escape from conversation with the gentleman, Lucy began walking at a bracing speed along the path. She intended to attain the house before he could question her too closely. Unhappily, his long strides enabled him easily to keep pace with her.

"In point of fact," she said, "I *was* thinking about you."

"No doubt you regret that you were too indisposed to walk out with me when I asked."

"I was told you had gone after the poachers."

"I caught them and sent them in Lord Knatchbull's care to the magistrate. So now I am come back to find you. How pleased I am to see that you are recovered from your late indisposition."

"I was not indisposed," she said truthfully. "I merely did not wish to walk with you." She hoped to ruffle his composure with this piece of directness. However, he remained unperturbed. Lucy walked faster. There were three walled gardens to pass through before she would reach the house.

"If I were not the mildest fellow in the world," he said mildly, "I might construe that as an insult. I am the one, after all, who is being imposed upon by an imposter. But you do not see me acting missish or refusing to walk out, do you?''

Abruptly she stopped to look at him, causing him to stop, as well. In a voice that impressed him with its earnestness, she asked, "Why do you support this charade? Why do you not expose me as an imposter?''

"By the same token, I might ask why you have chosen to *be* an imposter. What the deuce are you after?''

Pleased that she had piqued his curiosity after all, she said, "Mr. Hunt says you mean to offer me money.''

He laughed. "I mean to do nothing of the kind.''

"Then what do you mean to do?'' She could not help thinking that the miniature she had seen at his mother's house hardly did justice to his fine features.

"I mean to teach you what it is to be engaged to the Earl of Silverthorne," he said. She was studying his face, as if to penetrate the mystery of him, and instantly he was struck by the depth of blue in her eyes. The richness of colour was enhanced by the silver and blue of her bonnet ribbon, the red and blue of her pelisse, the purple and blue of the blossoms lining the path. Her nearness worked forcefully on him. Pulling her close, he kissed her, and when he felt her lips tremble under his, he became sensible of a hunger he had long thought dead. Having taught her the lesson he had intended, he might now have released her. Instead, his arms went round her, pressing her close.

The instant he touched her, Lucy felt a shock that left her helpless. It was some time before she recollected herself and could push him away, and a full minute before it occurred to her to be angry. She had raised her hand to smite his cheek when Lady Knatchbull appeared on the path, startling her.

Indeed, Lady Knatchbull startled herself by coming upon the two in the midst of an embrace. For the past month she had made it her careful study not to come upon Lord Roderick in tête-à-tête with one of his ladies. She said lightly, "Ah, you turtledoves must not heed an old woman on her way to the house. As you were, my dears. As you were." On that, she hurried along the path as quickly as she could.

Mortified to have been found in Lord Roderick's embrace, Lucy followed after her ladyship, saying breathlessly, "We should be delighted to have your company. Lord Roderick and I had finished our business, I assure you."

"I am sure you can invent more business," said Lady Knatchbull, hurrying.

"But we would not wish to exclude anyone from our conversation, and especially not our hostess."

"Miss Bledsoe, I do not object to lovers stealing kisses in my garden. They might be supposed to be overcome by the powerful nature of their affections from time to time. I ask only to be excused from witnessing it."

Panting with vexation as much as exertion, Lucy cried, "Wait. Please stop." She halted, trying to catch her breath. Lady Knatchbull stopped, as well.

Lucy looked around to ascertain his lordship's whereabouts and found to her alarm that he approached at a good pace. Turning to Lady Knatchbull, she began to defend her conduct, saying, "When you saw us kissing...that is to say, when you saw Lord Roderick kissing me... what I am trying to tell you is that I was not—" and here she stopped, for to say that she was not actually engaged to him and had had no more idea of being kissed than of being crowned queen would be to unmask herself. And to say that she had been insensible of the power of the kiss would be to lie.

"You were not what?" asked her ladyship helpfully.

Not knowing how to answer, and seeing Lord Roderick only steps from where she stood, Lucy felt trapped. Impulsively, she caught her bonnet in one hand, her skirt in the other and ran to the house.

LADY PHILPOTT WOULD NOT HEAR of their quitting Lever Combe, as Lucy suggested. In the first place, they had only just arrived, and if there was one thing she detested, it was swoofing about from place to place. She would not be so ill-mannered as to throw Lady Knatchbull's kind hospitality in her face; nor could she disappoint her dear friend Lady Roderick, who would be crushed should they return to Queenscroft without having done as they had promised in regard to her son. She urged Lucy to be patient and reminded her that she had agreed to spend a full fortnight endeavouring to teach him a lesson. Surely, Lucy was too honourable to go back on such a promise.

After the late encounter in the garden, Lucy suspected that Lord Roderick might well be impervious to all lessons of any kind. His kiss was proof that his insolence knew no bounds. Nevertheless, she was brought to agree with Lady Philpott. She would not to be driven away in defeat before she had outlasted one day. Furthermore, she would not permit fear of meeting Lord Roderick to keep her away from the roses. She had undertaken to teach the earl a lesson and teach him she would, and not merely because she would not go back on her promise to Lady Roderick. She would not go back on the promise she had made to herself: to test her mettle against a dyed-in-the-wool scoundrel and to come away unscathed.

Thanks to Lady Knatchbull's thoughtfulness, Lucy was placed at dinner next to Lord Roderick. As he held her chair for her, he remarked that she was in very great beauty that evening. Tittering behind her fan, she blinked fetchingly and said he had no doubt paid that same compliment to every lady in the room. With a pleasant smile, he confessed that he had.

When she felt him admire her bare neck and bosom, set off prettily by a white puff-sleeved sarcenet, she rapped him on the hand with her fan and called him a "naughty, naughty man." His response was merely a smile, which, like the smile in his miniature, struck Lucy as perilous. She warned herself to be careful.

Because Lady Knatchbull had invited a number of country families to dine, the hall was festive with laughter, candlelight and the aroma of exquisite dishes. Lucy admired the long table and the company. His lordship admired her. She felt his eyes upon her earring, a blood-red garnet in gold filigree, and she felt certain that her ear and neck must soon turn the colour of the gem if he continued his staring very much longer. No one, not even Sir Vale Saunders, had ever made her as uneasy as the Earl of Silverthorne.

Ignoring his plate of baked turbot, he watched her eat hers, saying when she had finished, "What a fortunate fillet, to be brought continuously to your lips."

She favoured him with an innocuous remark on the late rains.

"That will not do for an answer, my sweet," his lordship said.

Smiling, she replied, "Excessive gallantry must be answered with an observation on the weather. It deserves no more."

With feigned shock, he responded, "You do not think me insincere, I hope. I assure you, from what I tasted of your lips, that fish on your plate is in truth a lucky fellow."

"You would please me more by eating him, sir, than by envying him."

Speaking softly in her ear, he said, "I hope you are not angry with me on account of the kiss. You are, after all, my betrothed. Surely you would not have accepted my proposal if you did not like me a little. I do not approve of marriages of convenience, you know; not that I approve of *in*convenient marriages, either. But I do think a lady ought to like, if she cannot love, her companion through life."

Unsettled by his nearness, Lucy took a moment to collect herself. She scarcely knew how to answer him, for no matter what she said, it egged him on to further impertinence. There was only one thing for it, she thought: the bald truth. Taking a breath for courage, she said steadily, "I agree. One ought to like the man to whom one is engaged. That is why it is pity I do not like you."

He sat back in his chair, surprised. No woman had ever disliked him. The sensation was entirely new, and not a little amusing. It challenged him to charm her. "Well, I shall make you like me," he said.

"That would be punishment indeed!" she replied. "You see, I do not wish to like you."

His good nature was unflagging. "Ah, then I appear to be doing exactly as I thought: giving you the pleasure of disliking me." But although he continued to smile blandly, he had to acknowledge privately that her pointed dislike intrigued him.

After the fish course was removed and the cherried duck served out, Lucy turned her attention to Owen Hunt, asking him whether he had been pleased with the lyme walk. When they had sufficiently exhausted this subject, she had to ransack her mind for another. It was an arduous task to concentrate on conversation, for she often felt his lordship's arm brush hers as he ate. Soon she gave up the effort at conversation and turned her attention to the braised fowl.

"Tell me, dearest bride," said Lord Roderick in her ear, "Am I not a fine specimen? Am I not what is referred to in current parlance as a 'catch'? Do you not go about telling the world that we are to be married?"

Lucy paused before bringing the fork to her lips. "Yes," she said truthfully.

"Then I should like to know why you say you do not like me."

"I'm afraid you will not be pleased with my reason."

"Nevertheless, I wish to know."

Mustering her courage, she said, "Well, the truth is, you are a scoundrel, sir."

The epithet entertained him. "What is that to the purpose, my love? No woman ever disliked a man for being a scoundrel. In my experience, she likes him the better for it."

Here Lucy saw her opportunity to teach the lesson she had come to impart. Taking a breath and clearing her throat, she stated, "It is unfortunate that your self-interest prompts such a view. However, you must be aware that it does not hold true for every female. *I*, for example, do not like a scoundrel. I cannot esteem a man who makes love to a great many women at once and then, when they quite naturally think of matrimony, invents an engagement to fob them off."

He set down his fork and knife, amused that she knew so much about him. "You appear to have made a study of me," he said. His smile broadened. "I find it interesting that you should study a man you despise. Perhaps you do not despise me as much as you say." On that, he reached for her hand, which had rested in her lap.

As soon as he took her hand, the confidence that had filled her began to melt. Keeping her breath steady, she said, "You must let go, sir. Otherwise I shall inadvertently knock this duck onto your coat. To be sure, it is a very fine coat and is certain to be stained beyond help by the sauce."

He placed his other hand on hers, smiling impudently into her eyes. "You are incapable of having such an unfortunate accident. You are far too elegant. Moreover, as your betrothed, I may take certain liberties and all the world is obliged to indulge them, especially you, my beauteous bride-to-be."

Glancing around for some means of escape, Lucy tried to catch the eye of Lady Philpott. But her ladyship sat across the table regaling her host with a receipt for curing toothache, and the winking candles and the pyramids of plums and apricots in the centre of the table shielded Lady Philpott from all entreaties.

All at once, Lucy felt helpless. It struck her that she was no match for Lord Roderick, any more than she had been a match for Sir Vale. In spite of her struggle to be calm, her eyes filled. Unsteadily she said, "I beg you, do not flirt with me, sir. I do not know how to flirt. I do not know how to banter with you. You are too clever for me."

The seriousness in her tone caught him. Slowly, he brought her hand to his lips, kissed her palm, then let it go. Turning to his dinner once more, he saw the others watching him with undisguised curiosity. "Miss Bledsoe and I have had a lovers' quarrel," he announced amiably, "but it is no cause for you to stop eating. I recommend the potatoes. There is nothing I see so rarely or enjoy so well at my dinner as potatoes which have been roasted to a turn."

Although the guests soon resumed eating, Lucy could not be tranquil. Lord Roderick's quizzing had put her in a high state of emotion. How would she contrive to teach the scoundrel a lesson if she could not even contrive to meet his eyes, return his sallies or laugh at his gallantries?

Lord Roderick made no further attempt to induce Miss Bledsoe to like him. It surprised him to know just how much he wished her to like him, but it surprised him even more to know that his efforts to make her do so put her off all the more. There was only one way to deal with such a female—a method that had never failed him in the past.

Accordingly, with noble forbearance, on which he congratulated himself many times, he refrained from speaking to her throughout the remainder of the dinner. When the ladies withdrew afterwards, and the gentlemen joined them half an hour later, the earl made sure to seat himself at the opposite end of the saloon from where Miss Bledsoe sipped coffee. Lady Philpott beckoned to him several times and even winked at him once in an effort to lure him to Lucy's side, but he virtuously declined.

Instead he invited Miss Miranda Crowther-Biggs to join him at the pianoforte for a little music. If she would favour them with "Begone, Dull Care," he would turn the pages for her. Miranda was so grateful to be singled out that she forgot to be angry with the gentleman. Smiling triumphantly, she allowed herself to be escorted to the instrument. Sitting on a sofa across the room, Lucy watched. Soon her attention wandered to Owen Hunt, who stared at Miss Crowther-Biggs in lovesick dejection.

It was the earl's intention to pique Lucy's jealousy with his attention to Miranda. In this endeavour, he estimated that he was making good progress, because Miss Bledsoe regarded him with an expression of the deepest sorrow. Delighted with his success, he increased his assiduities to Miranda.

Meanwhile, Lucy contrived to engage Mr. Hunt in conversation, and it did not take above two minutes for her to ascertain that Miss Crowther-Biggs, who was basking in the glow of Lord Roderick's attention, was the object of the young man's passion. Every time the earl selected a new song for the girl or exchanged a smile with her or whispered in her ear, Mr. Hunt winced. Lucy's heart went out to him, especially as it seemed that Lord Roderick was deliberately flaunting his attentions to Miranda in the cruelest manner.

At the end of the evening, they all stood to say their good-nights, and as they passed through the doors on their way to the stairs, Roderick could not resist pausing in the shadows of the grand staircase to say to Lucy, "You cannot dislike me so much as you did. I have given you what required a good deal of sacrifice on my part, namely, my absence." He expected her to have missed his attentions enough to appear more in charity with him than she had earlier. Moreover, he was confident that the dim chandelier light which played so exquisitely on her face also set off his handsome looks to advantage.

Nothing in her expression, however, bespoke a desire to be made love to. Indeed, as she looked at him, he read the most earnest distress in her face. "You are breaking Mr. Hunt's heart!" she said passionately. "Surely even *you* cannot be so unfeeling as to betray your friend."

CHAPTER FIVE

Proof of the Pudding

HIS LORDSHIP COULD NOT IMAGINE what she was talking about. Nor did he have the opportunity of finding out, for she disappeared up the stairs in the wake of Lady Philpott. Like the others, he retired to his chamber, but not to sleep. He spent the night wondering who this bewitching woman was, what she wanted, why she had pleaded with him, where the deuce Owen Hunt fit into it all and how he might contrive to kiss her again.

On the morrow, he sought out Lucy in the breakfast parlour. The instant he entered, she coloured and rose to leave. The eyes of the others were fixed on them, watching as he said, "I must speak with you, o, love of my life."

Lucy answered with a gaiety audible throughout the room, "Alas, I am promised to drive out with Lord Knatchbull."

With the sweetest of smiles, he whispered, "My darling Lucy, if you do not explain your outlandish accusation of last night, I shall tell everyone here that I am not engaged to you."

She smiled back and, with much less volume but no less gaiety than before, replied, "Then I shall tell everyone here that you are not engaged to *anyone*, and never have been."

He glanced around to see Cora St. John and Mrs. and Miss Crowther-Biggs studying his every move. Turning to Lucy with a laugh, he remarked, "What a charming threat. You are indeed a worthy consort for a scoundrel."

On that reply, Lucy hurried from the parlour, not because she was late for her appointment with Lord Knatchbull, but because she was not nearly as amused by that parting observation as his lordship.

Following her exit, Roderick addressed his audience, "Miss Bledsoe and I have not yet patched up our quarrel. However, I do not despair, for after she has tormented me for the allotted time, I shall make her a present of a diamond and be forgiven forthwith." While the women glared at him as though they would like to see his heart cut out and posted atop a pike on London Bridge, he hummed a tune and helped himself at the sideboard to pork chop, toast and egg with caper.

IT WAS LORD KNATCHBULL'S custom to drive out every morning with a lady who was not his wife. As Miss Bledsoe had not yet been thus honoured, he set forth with her in his phaeton and four under a hazy sky and discoursed upon toothache. At last, he observed kindly, "I am very sorry you and Roderick have quarrelled. Perhaps I may be of service to you. If you have any love notes or locks of hair to send, I recommend young Briggs, the footman, who is most discreet in delivering such items."

Lucy thanked the white-whiskered old gentleman but declined. "Indeed," she said, "it would be most ungenerous of me to repay your hospitality by embroiling you in our dispute."

Enchanted with her blue eyes and silk bonnet, he vowed he wished to see her happy. "For I was young once myself," he recollected. "While I courted Lady Knatchbull, we enjoyed many a quarrel. On one occasion she nearly boxed my ears."

Lucy smiled.

"I suppose she did it for the same reason you have fallen out with Roderick—jealousy. You do not like his being such a favourite with the ladies. But you must not take his behaviour amiss, my dear. He is, after all, a man, and men cannot help loving a great many ladies. It is, alas, our fate."

With gentle archness, Lucy replied, "It must be very hard, knowing one is fated to love so many ladies and be boxed on the ears for it."

"Oh, it is, it is," he said with a sigh, and would have elaborated on the numerous hardships he himself had experienced, but the left wheel of the phaeton ran into a mud hole and sank several inches. His lordship leaned to the side to observe the calamity. Then, looking on high, he saw that the sun's good cheer had been replaced by a lowering cloud, one that promised to pour rain upon himself and his elegant companion. He lost no time in responding to this unhappy turn of events with a groan.

Alighting, he attempted to lead the horses forward and thus coax the wheel from its lodging place, but when it began to drizzle, he foresaw that he must set about raising the hood of the phaeton. With Lucy's help, he succeeded, so that they had shelter for their heads. Then he sat down by her side with another groan. "We shall have to wait here until someone comes for us," he declared.

"Do you think someone will come?" Lucy asked, more concerned that his lordship was miserable than that she would soon be soaked to her skin.

"Certainly someone will come. Someone is sure to observe that we are missing. Surely Lady Knatchbull will notice. Meanwhile, we must snuggle cosy, and not let the rain ruin your pretty shoes."

The rain came full force now. Because she did not wish to "snuggle cosy" with her host and because she was in a fair way to being drenched anyway, Lucy saw no reason to sit idly. She therefore evaded his lordship's protective arm and climbed down to see whether she might induce the conveyance forward by leading the horses.

"You will soil your dress," Lord Knatchbull warned.

Lucy soon found that the rain had sufficiently loosened the mud in the hole to release the wheel. Carefully, she led the horses round to face in the opposite direction, but despite her care, she could not avoid muddying her yellow dress, purple pelisse, black boots and rosy face.

When she had joined Lord Knatchbull in the phaeton again, he started the horses, whispering, "You need not say anything about this to Lady Knatchbull, you know. Perhaps she will not see us come in and will never be the wiser."

Lucy promised to keep mum and thought that, in future, she would not ride out with her host without making preparations for catastrophe. She was still smiling over this wisdom when she and Lord Knatch-

bull were met along the path by the Earl of Silverthorne's carriage, come in search of them.

Both equipages stopped in the grey rain. Lord
Roderick stepped from the carriage, opened an umbrella, and went to the phaeton to help Lucy down. As
he reached out a hand, he smiled at the sight of her.
Catching his expression, she became aware that the
wet muslin of her dress clung to her legs. To hide her
blush, she put a hand to her cheek and smeared it with
mud. At that moment, her purple bonnet feather col-
lapsed over her forehead.

Cautiously she stole a glance at Lord Roderick and
found him regarding her with an expression of such
intensity that she was caught off guard. She had
expected him to laugh at her as he laughed at everything. Not only was he not laughing, but, judging
from the glow of his eyes, he was not even conscious
that she appeared perfectly ridiculous.

Taking her by the waist, he swung her down from
the phaeton. Then, gravely, he removed the limp
feather from her brow.

The footman, who had finished rescuing Lord
Knatchbull, handed Roderick a fur, which he wrapped
tightly around Lucy, and as their eyes met, she could
not help smiling. "I hope it does not shock your sensibilities, my lord, to see the future Countess of Silverthorne in such a muddy, bedraggled condition."

"No amount of mud and rain could mar your elegance, my love. I only wish I might have had it all to
myself on the ride back to the house." On that, he installed her in his carriage and did not leave her side
until they reached Lever Combe.

BECAUSE LADY PHILPOTT would not permit poor chilled Lucy to leave her bed, it was not until the following morning that the earl had any hope of seeing her. Missing her at breakfast, he searched for her through the house until he found her in the library.

The room was warm, with brown wainscotting, book-lined shelves, crimson chairs and old, dark tables, one of which bore a decanter of old, dark wine. A single beam of sunlight, streaming in through a high casement window, penetrated the chamber.

Lucy's pink muslin was the only splash of bright colour in the room. When she saw Lord Roderick enter the library, her thoughts leapt to their last encounter. Recollecting the appreciation in his eyes, she glanced down at her book.

"Ah, my angel," he said pleasantly, "I have found you at last. I perceive you have recovered from your delightful drive with Lord Knatchbull. No young lady, I am happy to report, has died of one yet."

Turning a page, she said, "Yes, I have recovered, thank you, but I'm afraid his lordship has a vile cold."

An awkward pause ensued, during which she felt his eyes on her. He moved closer to say, "Miss Bledsoe, if you are going to do me the honour of accusing me of betraying a friend, you might at least give me an explanation."

She glanced up from her volume of *The Tatler* to ask with concern, "Do you really have no idea how much Mr. Hunt suffers?" She studied his face as though it were the page of a book that needed close reading to be understood.

"How do you imagine I have caused him to suffer?" he enquired, taking another step closer.

"You have made Miranda Crowther-Biggs fall in love with you." Then, turning her blue eyes on him, she added, "Surely you know how much that wounds your friend."

He took the book out of her hand and closed it, an act of high-handedness that caused Lucy to flush. "I am relieved to find," he said, "that there is nothing at all in what you say. When I first heard it, I confess, I was a trifle alarmed. But now I am reassured, for I have not the least interest in Miss Crowther-Biggs. As to Owen, you imply that he has conceived a tendre for the girl. In point of fact, he has too much sense to esteem such a simpering little hussy." As if to emphasize the lack of substance in her charge, he tossed her book on a chair.

Lucy was more unsettled than ever by his lordship's insouciance. It appeared to her a disturbing mixture of arrogance and charm. Stepping back a bit so that she would not be distracted by his nearness, she said, "I know it may be difficult for you to believe, for you evidently do not hold the young lady in very great esteem, but I am convinced Mr. Hunt is in love with her."

"Your conviction is charming, to be sure, but I do not think one may know anything about another human creature after scarcely a week's acquaintance, not even in these lax times."

"I do not know how to persuade you that I am not joking, sir. Mr. Hunt is in a fair way to having his heart broken, and though nobody dies of a broken heart, please believe me when I say that they do suffer."

Regarding her, he said softly, "It really is too bad, you know."

"Yes, Mr. Hunt is quite wretched, I fear."

"I am speaking of us, Miss Bledsoe. It really is too bad that you do not like me, for I like you very much."

Lucy felt her heart constrict.

Smiling, he placed a gentle finger on her cheek. Then, abruptly, he retrieved her book, placed it in her hand, opened to a page and, with a stylish bow, left her to her studies.

SHE SAW NO MORE of his lordship until Evensong. He entered the church during the first reading and took a seat in a pew behind the others. When the worshippers raised their voices to sing "All Praise to Thee," Lucy turned to catch a glimpse of him. Nodding, he favoured her with a highly impious smile.

After the service, he walked back to the house with Miranda Crowther-Biggs, while Lucy walked between Lord Knatchbull and Lady Philpott. Her two companions were pleased to continue their discussion of cures for toothache. Lucy approved the topic because it was one that did not require her to listen, much less speak. Thus, she was at liberty to observe his lordship as he made a grand flourish and invited Mr. Hunt to join him in escorting Miss Crowther-Biggs along the lyme walk.

The actions of the three just ahead of her roused Lucy's curiosity. After some minutes, Lord Roderick paused to consult his watch in the dim twilight. When he indicated that he was ready to proceed, a shift of positions took place. Instead of walking in the middle, he walked next to Mr. Hunt. This manoeuvre placed Owen next to Miranda, so that the young man was obliged to offer her his arm.

Lucy could see that Lord Roderick spoke rapidly, and though she could not make out his words, he evidently entertained his companions hugely. She then saw his lordship poke an elbow into his friend's side, which caused Mr. Hunt to jump and then incline his head to Miss Crowther-Biggs in order to address some remark to her. The upshot of this exchange was that Mr. Hunter was given the honour of carrying Miss Crowther-Biggs's prayer book. Lucy was intrigued by this little drama. It appeared to her that the earl had engineered the entire proceeding.

The party now reached the end of the lyme walk, where the door in the brick wall led to the gardens. At this juncture, Lucy witnessed another shift of position. Lord Roderick stood by the open door to let his companions pass through, but he did not follow them. Instead, he waited for her and her companions, and as she passed him, he said, "Miss Bledsoe, do you not think a library an excellent place? One learns so much there that one never knew before. I vow, I am thinking of renouncing dissipation and devoting myself entirely to scholarship."

Before Lucy could answer in the same style, Lady Philpott rapped the earl on the arm and informed him that if he was going to bore them with talk of libraries, nobody of fashion would have anything to do with him. He had better walk back to the house with herself and Lucy, and he must bestir himself to talk about something sensible.

Bowing with characteristic geniality, the earl gave one arm to her ladyship and the other to Miss Bledsoe, who, Lady Philpott noted with pleasure, took it with a very good grace.

AT THE HOUSE, the party was greeted by Cora St. John
and Mrs. Crowther-Biggs, who had begged off at-
tending Evensong and now complained bitterly of ennui. Ennui was the last of Lucy's complaints. She was
finding Lord Roderick a subject of consuming interest. Every day, every hour, she was becoming more
aware of his powerful presence. Moreover, she was
burning to know what he meant by manoeuvring Mr.
Hunt to walk with Miss Crowther-Biggs. However, she
was soon forced to give her thoughts another direction, for a commotion was heard outside the saloon
and shortly thereafter a stranger entered.

Red-faced, puffing and very much in his cups, the
newcomer searched until his eyes rested upon Cora St.
John. That lady rose, threw a stricken look at Lord
Roderick and murmured, "Mr. Turcott, why did you
not tell me you meant to come?"

The man grinned loosely. "I wished to surprise you,
my love. And I see I have."

It took Lucy less than an instant to conclude that
Mr. Turcott was a dreadful fellow. Not only did his
unexpected appearance cause the entire company to
gape at him and to fidget with uneasiness, but he
stank. From where she sat, she inhaled the essence he
gave off of stables, tobacco and brandy. In addition,
he looked from Cora St. John to Lord Roderick and
back again in a coarse, ugly way which frightened her.

In the face of such boorishness, Lady Knatchbull
summoned up only enough politeness to make per-
functory introductions. Turcott received the announcement of names with a yawn, until Lucy was
presented to him. Upon hearing that the young lady
with the blue eyes was Lord Roderick's betrothed, he
kneaded his brows suspiciously and looked her over as

though she were a mare on display at Tattersall's. "What, do you mean to shackle yourself to a blackguard?" he demanded.

The question set everyone on edge. Its tone was so insinuating, so openly insulting, that Lady Knatchbull began to fear a duel would be the result. Lord Roderick came close to the man and was about to seize him by the collar when Lucy stood up and smiled at the newcomer. Her elegance awed him a little, as did her curtsying to him in the most respectful manner and saying, "Indeed he is my betrothed, sir, and I beg you will wish me happy." Her blue eyes regarded him so softly that he was obliged to reply somewhat sheepishly that of course he wished her happy. He was not so mean a fellow, he declared, that he would refuse to wish a pretty young miss very happy. Before he could add that he doubted whether she would be happy with such a flat as Roderick, Lucy stretched out her hand to him, saying, "You must come and tell me all about your journey hither, for there must have been many little adventures along the way." Then she led him to the sofa, which Mr. Hunt and Miranda instantly vacated, and entreated him to sit with her.

During the next twenty minutes, Lucy had listened to a rendition of every detail of Turcott's journey to Lever Combe. The description included the price of a roasted joint and two bottles of wine at the Tunbridge Arms, the insolence of the ostlers, the pitiful performance of his horses whom he had a good mind to shoot and a thousand other complaints.

As she heard him out, Lucy thought back over what she had just done. Her feelings were in turmoil, so that it took her a while to clarify her motives for jumping up to greet Mr. Turcott with such alacrity and engaging him in their present interminable and decidedly one-sided conversation.

She realized that as soon as he had entered, she had sensed danger. The danger had been felt by everyone, or nearly everyone—Lord Knatchbull and Lady Philpott were still engrossed in toothache. The threatening glares Mr. Turcott had shot at Lord Roderick had alarmed her; his expression, as he looked from Cora St. John to the earl, struck her as murderous. It implied that he suspected an illicit affair of the heart was going forward right under his nose. What frightened Lucy more than anything was that she shared this suspicion. Cora St. John had not troubled to hide her interest in Lord Roderick, nor her jealousy where Lucy was concerned.

In fact, Lucy suspected that there was not a female under Lady Knatchbull's roof, not even Lady Knatchbull herself, who was not enamoured to some degree or other with the earl—herself excepted, of course. She had guessed from her observations and some hints dropped by Lord Knatchbull that Roderick was conducting simultaneous amours with the betrothed of Mr. Turcott, the wife of Mr. Crowther-Biggs and the beloved of Owen Hunt. Given what she knew about the gentleman, she was not surprised. But she had feared that Turcott would do harm; consequently, she had leapt into the breach.

She now wished she had not done anything so rash. Not only had she aided the very man she wished to teach a lesson, protecting him from the consequences of the very conduct she despised, but *she* was now being punished. It was she, not Roderick, who was forced to hear Turcott's muling complaints. Indeed, by listening to him, she had induced the fellow to take a liking to her. He was not only grinning at her in the lewdest manner, but breathing his foul breath on her and patting her hand so that his might occasionally brush her knee.

LORD RODERICK did not understand why Miss Bledsoe had put herself between him and Turcott, but the action did not surprise him. Indeed, nothing that young lady did surprised him any longer. She was as intelligent, lovely and elegant as he had first thought. And she had discovered in a short time what he had failed to discern entirely, that his friend Owen Hunt was incurably in love with one of the most brainless girls in Britain.

His glance fell on his friend and the girl as they stood by the fireplace, admiring a painted plate. Just then, Miranda happened to look at his lordship. She gazed at him with an expression dripping with tenderness. Now he saw that he ought to have discouraged the young creature from the first, from the night she had waylaid him in the conservatory. Her expression was the same his spaniel bestowed upon him whenever he returned from his travels. It was the same look which Owen Hunt was bestowing at this very minute upon Miranda. In short, it was proof of the pudding that Miss Bledsoe knew his friend's heart better than he did.

Well, he must set things right with Owen. Not that he thought it would be a very good thing if Miranda returned his affection. But if that was what his friend wished, then he must see to it.

Accordingly, he turned his back to Miranda and sat down by her mother, with whom he flirted relentlessly for the remainder of the evening. From time to time, he caught sight of Miranda wiping a tear. He saw Owen offer her his linen and lead her solicitously to a sofa. He saw Owen do his utmost to comfort her, and he saw that his plan was already succeeding in bringing the two young people together.

Excellent, he thought. Let Miranda Crowther-Biggs forget about snaring an earl. Let her love Owen Hunt with all her heart, such as it was. And then, for Owen's sake, let her jilt him without mercy.

THE FOLLOWING MORNING, Lucy went along the path through the gardens in search of Mr. Turcott, who had extracted from her a promise to show him the roses. Twice she stopped to inspect the clouds overhead and to wonder if a rain shower might be counted on to cancel the tour. When she passed through three of the gardens without finding him, she began to hope that the gentleman had forgotten the appointment and started back to the house. A loud shriek from the next garden, however, caused her to stop. Moving to the vine-covered brick archway, she peeked inside.

At the sound of another shriek, she went into the garden. In a small temple of graceful white columns, Mr. Turcott struggled with Mrs. St. John. The lady had fallen to her knees. The gentleman was trying to pull her to her feet.

Impulsively, Lucy started forward to intervene. As she approached, she saw Turcott shake Mrs. St. John, so that the widow covered her ears with her hands and sobbed. Lucy reached them in time to stop the man from inflicting further harm.

Turcott tipped his hat to Lucy, explaining, "I've had to teach the woman what it means to be engaged to Desmond Turcott. I vow you would not blame me if you knew the entire tale.''

"Oh, but I would blame you," Lucy said. Her tone was so gentle and ladylike that the man did not catch her meaning.

He went on, saying, "I don't like to tell you all the reasons I have; it is not fit for the hearing of such a young lady as yourself. But trust a gentleman to know what is the way to keep a female on the right path.''

Lucy went to Mrs. St. John to help her to her feet. Cora declined at first, shaking her head, saying that she would only be knocked down again if she got up. Persistent and gentle persuasions, however, raised her at last. Fearfully the woman glanced at Turcott. He laughed to see her cower. Raising his hand, he feigned a cuffing. Lucy responded by placing herself in front of Cora.

Taken aback, Turcott stared.

Mrs. St. John tried to persuade her to come away, but Lucy was determined to remain where she was. "I ask you please not to frighten this poor creature any further, sir." Her voice was unsteady with emotion.

"And why should I not? She belongs to me, does she not? She is my property, or will be soon enough. It is the same thing, is it not? She has signed the contracts. Everything is arranged. She cannot undo it now.''

Lucy swallowed, then answered, "All the more reason why you should deal gently with her.''

He regarded her in bewilderment.

"It is the part of a gentleman," Lucy explained, "to be especially tender of the powerless.''

He laughed uproariously. "It is not Sunday, miss. I do not listen to sermons except of a Sunday.''

"You know very well it is wrong to treat Mrs. St. John in such a manner," she said in a voice that quavered in spite of her efforts.

Slapping his knee, he laughed. "And who's to stop me?"

In a low voice, Lucy replied, "I suppose I will if I must."

Enjoying the joke hugely, Turcott shrugged. "I do not wish to hurt you, miss. You are none of my belonging. But she is and you ought not interfere." He then turned to Cora St. John and directed a warning at her, "I hold you to your promises, Mrs. St. John. Do not think you can jilt me. Nor can you pay me to jilt you, so do not ever offer me your paltry bribes again. I said I would have you and I mean to do just that."

He seemed to contemplate a threat against Lucy, too, but restrained himself, and, tipping his hat once more to Lucy, he went away.

As soon as he was out of sight, Lucy looked to see what harm had been done to Cora St. John. Blood trickled from her ear. A worse calamity was her eye, which was beginning to show signs of bruising. Taking out her handkerchief, Lucy dabbed the ear. "We must go back to the house and see what the cook has to hand that might soothe that eye," said Lucy.

"Turcott was right. You ought not to interfere."

As Lucy chose not to confess how greatly she feared Turcott, she merely urged Mrs. St. John to come to the house at once.

"You are more of a fool than you know," Cora said harshly. "Roderick and I have been on terms of intimacy these many years."

Without flinching, Lucy said, "Yes, I guessed as much."

"What you have not guessed, however, and what I wish to tell you, is that I intend to have him. He may marry you, but he will belong to me."

Lucy did not doubt that the lady was telling the truth, and that certainty pained her. However, she said only, "If you do not care for that eye, you will be confined to your room for some days."

"I suppose I ought to thank you for coming to my rescue, but I cannot. Nothing is so galling as to be obliged to one's rival."

That epithet was too much. Losing the tenuous hold on her emotions, Lucy cried, "I am not your rival!"

"But you are engaged to him."

Lucy might have blurted out a hot denial had not Lord Roderick entered the garden at that moment. Seeing the ladies, he approached, smiled and raised his beaver. Then, noticing Cora's eye, he stopped smiling. Angrily he said, "What has he done this time?"

Cora sighed. "Not as much as he would have liked. Miss Bledsoe came along on her white horse and defended me from harm."

Grimly, Roderick studied Lucy. "I wish you had not done that. It was rash."

Seeing the gravity in his eyes, Lucy grew uncomfortable. She murmured, "The gentleman did me no harm."

His expression was dark. "In future, you will come to me, if you please, and I will see to the matter."

She stood up abruptly to face him. "You will see to the matter?" she said, exploding. "*You?* It is your fault to begin with that Turcott brutalizes Mrs. St. John."

He smiled. "I am pleased to see you rate my charms so high. I feared you were impervious to them altogether."

Nearly in tears, she implored, "Don't you see? It is your liaison with the lady that has made the man jealous. You are the reason he shakes and bruises her. If you mean what you say, if you truly wish to see to matters, then I beg you, leave this poor creature alone."

"You are a magnificent advocate," he said with unconcealed admiration.

Cora St. John, who never fancied a conversation that excluded her, rose and stood between them. To Roderick, she said, "I don't care a farthing if she is engaged to you, Roddy, I forbid you to listen to her." Then to Lucy, she said acidly, "Perhaps you should not ask Lord Roderick to leave me alone without first ascertaining whether I wish to be let alone. I hasten to assure you, Miss Bledsoe, I do not!"

CHAPTER SIX

A New View of the Matter

BECAUSE LADY KNATCHBULL had invited a number of the neighbourhood's best society to Lever Combe, the evening promised a good deal more amusement than the day had delivered. As Lucy had foreseen, the swollen eye kept Cora St. John confined upstairs. But the rest of the company was as convivial as Lady Knatchbull could have wished, even going so far as to applaud when some of the young people begged to be allowed to roll back the carpet so that couples might be formed for dancing.

Miranda Crowther-Biggs obliged the dancers by playing a succession of lively airs. Because Lord Roderick would not speak to or even look at her, she devoted all her attention to Mr. Hunt, who obliged her by turning pages. Lucy obliged herself by sitting where Mr. Turcott would not obtrude upon her sight. She entertained herself agreeably in conversation with a robust naval lieutenant, who ultimately prevailed upon her to join the set preparing to dance the reel.

When the dance was done, and the lieutenant had bowed himself off, Lady Knatchbull took Lucy aside to say, "It appears I did immeasurable harm by interrupting you and Lord Roderick in the garden that fateful morning. I can see now that you had been quarrelling, and had I not come along, you might have patched it up between you."

"Please do not reproach yourself," Lucy responded. "His lordship and I are on the same terms as we ever were."

"Ah, you wish to spare me self-reproach by saying so, but I am not to be hoodwinked. How can I ignore what is before my very eyes? Last night you did not speak a syllable to one another, and tonight, you sit on one side of the room flirting with a charming lieutenant, while his lordship stands on the other looking thoroughly bored."

Lucy glanced toward the earl to see him lounging against the doorpost, his arms folded. It seemed at first that he gazed at nothing in particular, stifling a yawn. On closer inspection, however, it proved that he studied Miranda and Mr. Hunt, who bent over to whisper a word to the adorable musician, a word that caused her to put her hands to her radiant cheeks.

The dancers cried out against the sudden musical void. Their complaints recalled the amorous Mr. Hunt to himself. Again he whispered to Miranda, who nodded at him with lingering looks and resumed playing, though she played so many wrong notes that the dancers began to cry out again.

Lucy concluded from this little scene that Mr. Hunt was rapidly improving his acquaintance with Miss Crowther-Biggs. The conclusion gratified her, given what she knew of the young man's feelings. She could not help looking at the earl to see how he bore up under the young woman's defection. He merely shrugged at the sight. Then he glanced so that his eyes met Lucy's. Suddenly he smiled, and with such impudence that she was obliged to look down. To Lady

Knatchbull she said, "My flirting with the lieutenant was harmless, ma'am. Lady Philpott says that it is vulgar to flirt with the gentleman one is engaged to."

"Very true, but you must make it up with Roderick. Although he is naughty, as you say, I have been brought to conclude since your arrival that you are the very wife for him. Under your gentle tutelage, he will learn to value a female worthy of being valued. Now come with me."

Before Lucy could protest, Lady Knatchbull drew her to where his lordship stood. "Here is Miss Bledsoe," she said to the earl. "She has come to make it up with you."

Lord Roderick said amiably, "From the expression she wears on her adorable face, I am quite certain Miss Bledsoe has no such intention. I begin to suspect she does not like being betrothed to me. Indeed, I think she means to cry off altogether."

"Cry off?" exclaimed Lady Knatchbull.

Lucy was caught by the playful light in his expression. Cora St. John might be furious with her after their late meeting, but he clearly was not. Smiling, she answered, "I shall not cry off, my lord. I shall not let you off so easily as that."

"Well done!" her ladyship declared. "Now everything will be right as rain again." Taking Lucy's hand, she placed it in Roderick's. "Here is her hand on the bargain," she announced.

Roderick looked solemnly at what he held, then just as solemnly at Lucy. When he detected a hint of amusement in the curve of her lips, he turned to Lady Knatchbull to say, "It pains me to contradict you, my lady, but this is not a hand."

"It most certainly is a hand! I believe I know a hand when I see one."

Gravely, he said, "This is a glove, not a hand."

"Well, if you are determined to split hairs, it is a hand in a glove."

"But you promised me the *hand* of my betrothed."

Lucy noted that, despite his complaint regarding her hand, he continued to hold it, and she was too curious to know what he would say next to snatch it away.

With a glance at Lucy's face, he began to remove her glove, beginning above the elbow and slowly uncovering her rosy arm as he inched the white silk towards him.

Lady Knatchbull fanned her neck and declared he was the naughtiest man she had ever beheld. Lucy thought that the room had grown remarkably warm and might have fanned herself, too, if her right arm had not already been engaged. She had often appeared in company bare-armed and bare-handed, but not until now had she felt so exposed.

She took a breath just as he finished taking off the glove. In fascination, she watched him bring it to his lips, fold it, place it in his breast pocket and swear to keep it by him always, or at least until he changed his coat.

"You are a dreadful man!" Lady Knatchbull scolded. "You cannot expect a lady to appear in society with only one glove. It is a perfect scandal."

Lucy smiled at him. "I should like his lordship to have the glove," she said. "Indeed, I have long been meaning to give him the glove."

Roderick laughed. "I see that Miss Bledsoe intends to challenge me to a duel—excellent preparation for marriage, I have no doubt."

Lady Knatchbull scoffed at the suggestion. "What is this nonsensical talk of duels? You must talk of dancing instead. Indeed, you must go and join the dance." Again she placed Lucy's hand—the bare one—in his lordship's.

Looking pointedly into her blue eyes, he said, "What do you say, Lucy, shall we leave off duelling in favour of a dance?"

It struck her that this was the first time she had heard him use her name. Its sound lingered in the air, warming her. After a pause, she went down to the dance on his arm, thinking to herself that there could not possibly be any harm in joining a set with a gentleman she would part from in a few days, never to see again.

For the next half hour, she was entertained with his opinions concerning the number of children he would expect her to bear him and the names and titles this army of offspring would be obliged to sport. As Lucy admired his laughing expression, it came home to her that in spite of all the warnings she gave herself, in spite of all her attempts to see his gallantries for the empty nothings they were, Lord Roderick exerted a powerful force on her, just as he did upon her entire gender. Try as she might, she could not help but be drawn to him. His magnetism put her greatly in mind of Sir Vale's.

At the recollection of Sir Vale, it suddenly occurred to her that she had given scarcely a thought to that gentleman since her arrival at Lever Combe. More than a week had passed without her once summoning up his face or hearing his voice. For the first time in what seemed like forever, she felt free of him.

The music stopped. Another cry went up from the dancers, who protested that Miss Crowther-Biggs put them off their steps with her faulty playing. Mr. Hunt asserted that they did the young lady an injustice, that they had wearied her to death by making her sit and play when she ought to have been dancing, too—or, at any rate, given a respite from her musical exertions. Other players were appealed to immediately. One of the married ladies from the village volunteered her services. But when the new set was formed, Lord Roderick procured a glass of wine for Lucy from a passing footman. Then he returned her to Lady Knatchbull.

"I am prodigiously fond of dancing," he explained. "It is the only means by which a gentleman may touch a lady without becoming either a husband or a scoundrel. Still, I must attend to other business." With a smile and a bow, he took himself off to his former place by the doorpost, from where, Lucy saw, he yawned and observed Owen Hunt and Miranda.

Looking in the same direction, Lucy saw Mr. Hunt assist Miranda to a chair, and bow. In another moment, he brought her a glass of lemonade. Sitting by her side, he whispered to her. Miss Crowther-Biggs's excitement was so great upon hearing his utterance that she upset her glass, spilling the drink on her thin white dress. Lucy could not shake the suspicion that the cause of the spilt drink was a proposal of marriage from the newly bold Mr. Hunt.

As soon as one of the ladies came to Miranda's aid, Mr. Hunt joined Lord Roderick. Lucy saw him tell the earl a tale which required much gesturing on his part. Impassively his lordship heard him out. When the tale was done, the earl clapped his friend on the shoulder.

Mr. Hunt then returned to Miranda, while Lord Roderick looked after him.

Having been patted dry, Miranda arranged herself adorably on the sofa. She received Mr. Hunt with a smile so full of sugar that Lucy began to wonder how Mr. Hunt could bear it. In any case, it was clear to Lucy that, sugary or not, Miranda was now as smitten with Mr. Hunt as he was with her, that the two appeared to deserve each other in every way, and that they might soon have an announcement to place in *The Times*. Another fact was clear to Lucy, as well: namely, that the two had been brought together by the manipulations of the Earl of Silverthorne, who from time to time glanced at the two lovers with a satiric expression.

Was it possible, Lucy wondered, that what she had said to Lord Roderick had affected him, that her reproofs had been heeded, that he had taken steps to right the wrong he had done Mr. Hunt? She would like to believe the answer was yes, but how could she? Why should Lord Roderick take to heart the opinions of a woman he had known so brief a time? He himself had told her that one could not know anything about another human creature in a week. All he had learned about her was that she was an imposter who disliked him. How was it possible that on such paltry information as that, he could not only credit what she said but go so far as to act upon it? She could not answer any of these questions, but at this moment, she felt a kinder sentiment towards him than she had ever done, and she thought of what he had done for Miranda and Mr. Hunt with the greatest of pleasure.

As she was savouring the sentiment, she found herself accosted by Mr. Turcott, who came close to her,

sending his breath over her bare neck and shoulder, to
say in a slur, "I have enquired about you, miss, and I
find you are a nobody. Your family have nothing but
respectability and lands in Ireland. You cannot do me
one jot of harm. And as to your betrothed, I am not
afraid of him, either."

Repressing her distaste, Lucy replied, "I never
threatened to do you harm."

He circled round and drew up a chair beside her. "I
have a notion to visit Mrs. St. John in her chamber. It
would not be the first time, you know. Tonight, she
prefers indulging a fit of the sullens to being in my
company, but I shall change her mind. If I cannot use
persuasions, I shall give her the lesson which you prevented me from concluding earlier today."

Lucy was too repelled to answer.

"Well," he challenged, "what have you to say to
that?"

She thought of a number of replies, none of which
her elegant education and breeding would permit her
to utter. Therefore, she remained in trembling silence, avoiding the man's eyes and breath as much as
she could.

"You were ready enough to rise to Mrs. St. John's
defence this afternoon. Perhaps you have come to
your senses since then. I am glad to see it." In an instant, he stood and walked from the saloon.

She could not permit him to carry out his threat. Yet
she was frightened of him, and had no hope of stopping him by herself. For an instant, she felt so angry
that she had an impulse to unpin an old pistol of Lord
Knatchbull's from its mountings on the wall and wave
it under Turcott's nose. But a more sensible solution
occurred to her the next moment. She would seek the

help of Lord Roderick, who knew the situation inti-mately and who would not be intimidated by Tur-cott's braggadocio.

He was still lounging by the door, watching Mir-anda and Mr. Hunt. Urgently she said, "Lord Rod-erick, I must speak with you."

"Ah, you have come for your glove, my heart's de-light. Your arm has grown chilled. Here, you must al-low me to warm it for you," he replied, and he reached for her hand.

"I've come to ask you to assist Mrs. St. John. Mr. Turcott has gone to her chamber, and I am afraid he means to do her mischief."

He did not stay another moment but, letting go of her hand, went immediately out of the room, making for the stairs, which he climbed two at a time. Lucy had no hope of keeping pace with him, but she fol-lowed as quickly as she could. The concern on his face as she had given him the news stayed in her mind. It was difficult to imagine a man of such relentless in-souciance feeling so much and permitting it to show. But she had caught him off guard. There was no time for him to be insouciant or even charming. Indeed, she liked him the better for not being charming at such a moment, for exiting without so much as taking proper leave in order to go at once to rescue someone in dis-tress. She liked him the better for not throwing it in her face that she had so recently implored him to leave Mrs. St. John alone. She liked him the better for trusting her so completely that he had not stayed to question. However, she did *not* like him the better for knowing so well the route to Cora St. John's bed-chamber.

Lucy arrived in time to find Mrs. St. John standing in the open door of her room, clinging to Lord Roderick, who caressed her soothingly. Her nightclothes were torn at the shoulder. She whimpered pathetically as she grasped him about the neck. Turcott was not to be seen.

With a pang, Lucy saw Roderick take the woman's hand and talk to her in a soft, comforting tone.

Cora St. John held on to him tightly. "I tried to break with him, Roddy, but he will not let me go. He says he will marry me whether I wish it or not."

Roderick would have answered, but looking up, he saw Lucy. By her pale colour and grave expression, he judged that she read a great deal into the situation. In her blue eyes, he saw both sympathy and disapproval. He liked the sympathy, which was all for Cora. Miss Bledsoe's generous heart was one of her most captivating qualities. And he was mused at the disapproval, which was all for him. Another of the lady's captivating qualities was that she disliked his being so well acquainted with so many ladies. It pleased him to think that she was liking it less and less every day.

Lucy was not certain what she ought to do, any more than she was certain what she ought to feel. The pain she experienced at the sight of Mrs. St. John in Roderick's arms dismayed her. Out of patience with her runaway emotions, she could do no more than favour the gentleman with a discreet nod and tiptoe down the corridor the way she had come, while he could do no more than follow her with his eyes.

IN THE MORNING, Lord and Lady Knatchbull were shocked to learn that Mr. Turcott had quit Lever Combe as unceremoniously as he had arrived. He had left no compliments for his host and hostess, or for his betrothed. According to the stablehand's report, he had ridden off in the dead of night with only the clothes he wore on his back, saying that he would send for his belongings later.

No one regretted the gentleman's departure. However, another departure took place that day which *was* regretted. Lord Roderick pleaded business in the north and left Lever Combe that afternoon. He did not say when he would return. Nor did he take leave of Lucy—not a word, a note, or even a look. His leaving so suddenly distressed her more than she could say.

Supper that night struck the entire company as singularly dull, and the evening's entertainment afterward was no better. Lord Roderick was gone, and in his place he had left two lovers who were more tiresome than the supper and the evening combined. Lady Knatchbull whispered to Lucy that no one was so insufferable as young people in love. Then, after a bit, she added, "Of course I do not refer to you and his lordship! You are a perfectly delightful pair of turtledoves."

Somewhat later in the evening, Lucy overheard Miss Crowther-Biggs say that Lord Roderick had left on account of her imminent engagement to Mr. Hunt. "He could not bear it," she confided to Lord Knatchbull in an audible whisper. "I'm afraid I've broken his heart." Hearing this explanation, Lucy smiled for the first time that day.

Mrs. Crowther-Biggs had another explanation for his lordship's sudden departure. "He cannot face me," she informed Lady Philpott. "He is sorry to have brought Miss Bledsoe here, as it forced me to sever all former ties of friendship and affection."

"His lordship did not send for Miss Bledsoe," Lady Philpott retorted. "The young lady came of her own accord. They had been separated far too long. Such a pity, too, for anyone can tell they are violently in love."

As this line of conversation was not altogether pleasing to Mrs. Crowther-Biggs, she soon excused herself to seek out her hostess.

Lucy would have liked to hear Cora St. John's explanation for the earl's departure, but as that lady did not stir from her room, there was no opportunity of asking. Earlier in the day, Lucy had sent a note enquiring after her health, but as yet she had received no reply. She guessed she would not receive one in the evening or, indeed, at all, for Cora St. John had made her jealousy perfectly plain.

Thus, Lucy retired for the night with no guess as to Lord Roderick's reason for quitting Lever Combe so unexpectedly. All she could say for certain was that she did not believe his departure was the result of a broken heart inflicted by the disaffection of either Mrs. Crowther-Biggs or her daughter, and that if he did not return soon, she might not see him again, as their fortnight's stay was nearly at an end.

LADY PHILPOTT HAD GONE more than ten days now without paying a visit to a single shop. Such deprivation rendered her nervous in the extreme. She had no hope that the village nearby afforded any better shopping than Canterbury. Still, an unsatisfactory purchase was better than no purchase at all. Therefore, her ladyship declared her intention of making do.

To the village they went, and while her ladyship lamented the paucity of modern facades on the houses,

Lucy took in the cheerful noises of the drays, the amiable greetings of the villagers and the bustling atmosphere of the town. The sights and sounds reminded her of her own village, Cheedham in Worcestershire, and for the first time since she had left it many months ago, she missed it. How very much she would have liked to return home. But her father had closed up the house when he had taken her brother to Brighton.

This reverie was interrupted by the arrival of Mr. Hunt. He was alone, Miss Crowther-Biggs having gone with her mother to be fitted for a gown, and there was no one he would rather see at this moment, he said, then Miss Bledsoe. Lady Philpott, who spied a silversmith's shop across the road, quickly excused herself. Left alone with the gentleman, Lucy observed his animated face.

"I wished you to know," he said shyly, "that Miss Crowther-Biggs has done me the honour of accepting my hand in marriage."

"Indeed," said Lucy, endeavouring to appear surprised.

"I wished particularly to tell you on account of the conversation we had shortly after your arrival."

"Yes, I recall your saying that you fancied yourself a little in love."

"I also said that I believed she did not love me because she was in love with Lord Roderick. I ought never to have said it. It was very wrong of me."

Lucy looked gently at him. "But it was true, wasn't it?"

He coloured. "Roderick cannot have been kinder. I owe him all my late good fortune. Indeed, some days ago he came to me to say that he had lately noticed my interest in Miss Crowther-Biggs. It indicated, he thought, a depth of affection he had not before witnessed in me. He asked me straight out whether I was in love with her, and when I confessed the truth, he did everything in his power to help me win her.''

"Did he?" It gladdened Lucy's heart to hear Mr. Hunt corroborate what she had suspected.

"Oh, yes. He could not have been more generous, though he did feel it his duty to point out that the young lady was very, very young and not as serious as myself.''

"I had not thought his lordship attended so assiduously to his duty. Perhaps I have done him an injustice.''

"He asked me what it was that would make me happy and naturally, I answered that to have Miss Crowther-Biggs would render me the happiest man on earth, and so he said he would do his best to see that I got her.''

Smiling, she said, "Lord Roderick doesn't waste a moment once he makes up his mind to a thing, and the upshot is that you are engaged. I wish you very happy.''

"Thank you, and now I feel impelled to ask you— and I do beg your pardon for so asking—please, Miss Bledsoe, go away.''

Astonished at this request, she laughed.

But, as usual, Mr. Hunt was as serious as death. "I beg you to quit Lever Combe. More than a week has passed and you still have not said what you mean to do about his lordship and this pose of yours. Now, because of what Roderick has done for me in regard to Miss Crowther-Biggs, I am obliged to make an equal show of friendship.''

"I hope it is only your loyalty to Lord Roderick which prompts this invitation."

"Oh, yes, I bear no grudge against you personally. In all other respects, I think you are quite delightful. But Roderick is very good, too, you know, though he would never wish me to say so. He makes it a point to be very bad. I daresay it is what renders him so charming to the ladies."

Lucy lowered her eyes. "I daresay you are right."

"I ask you to forget whatever scheme you have in mind and leave him alone. If money will persuade you, you have only to say so. If you prefer letters of introduction, an entrée into Society, either or both may be arranged. Only do not persist in plaguing him."

Lucy smiled and said that as it happened she would in all probability be leaving before the week was out.

At this announcement, Mr. Hunt looked so pleased that she could not forbear wondering whether Lord Roderick would receive the news with equal joy.

THE MORE LUCY THOUGHT about his late conduct, the more pleased she grew with Lord Roderick. What Mr. Hunt had confided to her had confirmed her earlier thoughts. Indeed, she had begun to see the earl in a different light. Lord Roderick was clearly not incorrigible; he was more than merely a handsome gallant, entirely devoid of character. He was capable of doing right.

Lucy felt sure that he had not liked the task of bringing together Mr. Hunt and his young lady, but he had done it nonetheless, to gratify his friend. That sort of consideration spoke well for him. Moreover, it marked the distinction between him and Sir Vale. The latter never gave another human creature consideration unless he proposed somehow to gain by it.

As to the matter of Cora St. John, Lucy allowed that the lady had certainly played a role there and one could not lay the entire blame for Turcott's jealousy at Lord Roderick's door.

So in charity was she with the earl that she vowed to say something to him when next they met. After all, she had told him that she disliked him and regarded him as a scoundrel. Now that she had seen some sign of the gentleman in him, she was obliged to be equally candid.

She was a little in dread of his interpreting the compliment as a hint to flirt with her, but she would take the risk. Surely one might pay a gentleman a compliment without repenting of it later. The prospect of seeing him again now filled her with anticipation.

CHAPTER SEVEN

Elopement

LUCY REMAINED PLEASED with his lordship until the next day, when she came upon Cora St. John near the acacia tree that had been the recent scene of Mr. Turcott's brutality. Because she knew that Mrs. St. John did not like her, Lucy hesitated before greeting her. Then, taking courage, she approached and asked after her health.

"I am well enough" came the curt reply. "The bruise does not heal quickly, but I manage to hide it somewhat."

Lucy asked whether she had received any word of Mr. Turcott.

"I do not expect to hear anything," said Cora. "He comes and goes as he likes. I have nothing to say to anything."

The lady had not invited Lucy to sit; therefore, she continued to stand. The leaves of the tree provided shelter from a grey day that had begun to drizzle. "Lord Roderick left us all very suddenly, did he not?" she said by way of opening. Her intention, she told herself, was merely to make unexceptionable conversation.

Cora smiled at her knowingly. Lucy's casual reference had not concealed her interest. "So he did not tell you where he has gone?'' she asked. "He did not tell even you!''

Lucy coloured. "He let it be known only that he was going into the north,'' she replied.

"He told *me* where he was going, but he did not tell *you*, the lady who is to be his bride,'' Mrs. St. John gloated.

Lucy did not betray her discomposure but said only, "Evidently he places a high degree of confidence in you.''

Cora produced a harsh laugh. "He has gone to find me a hiding place. When he returns, we shall go there together.''

Shocked, Lucy did not reply.

"Well, I cannot stay here or go back to London, can I? Turcott will be worse than ever now. Besides, Roderick will not allow me to return to London. He says I shall be in danger, and he will not have it. He says we must go away until Turcott comes to his senses and agrees to let me go.''

"I see.'' Lucy felt deflated, as though all the kind thoughts she had cherished lately regarding the earl had been merely the spinnings and weavings of her own fancy.

Disdainfully, Cora asked, "Is that all you have to say? 'I see'? I am about to elope with the man you are to marry, Miss Bledsoe. Surely you have something more to say than 'I see.' ''

With considerable restraint, Lucy confessed, "I am disappointed.''

"That will do for a start, though I must say, it is rather lukewarm. I do not know how Roderick came to engage himself to such an icicle as you. No wonder he wishes to take me away and make me his mistress."

Lucy bowed her head. "You are mistaken if you think I feel nothing. But I see no point in playing a Cheltenham tragedy over it. What you say does not surprise me in the least. Knowing what Lord Roderick is, I quite expected it."

"Well, I confess I did not expect you to take the news so well. You are not a bad sort of girl, really, and I suppose that I do not mind if this elopement of mine does not absolutely break your heart."

This reference to her broken heart stung Lucy as none of Mrs. St. John's intentional gibes had succeeded in doing. Consequently, she spoke with considerable passion when she answered, "I have no intention of breaking my heart, ever again. And as to my taking your news so well, I assure you it is nothing. How the Earl of Silverthorne chooses to conduct himself towards his female acquaintance is no concern of mine."

After a moment of observation, Cora St. John smiled and said slyly, "Yes, I can see very well that it is no concern of yours!"

Too distressed to notice this irony, Lucy cried, "I took Lord Roderick for a scoundrel the instant I heard his name, and what you have said only proves my impression. I am vindicated. There is nothing, nothing in the world, that can gratify one so profoundly and so delightfully as the knowledge that she has been right."

LUCY SAT DOWN on her soft, blue-covered bed. Lady Philpott sat nearby in a clawfooted chair, pinning a feather onto a hat of red silk. "I fear that Lord Rod-

erick's situation is even worse than we had foreseen,''
Lucy said.

''I am sure you take too gloomy a view, dear girl. A
man as handsome as he is must learn his lesson in good
time.''

''I doubt there will be time,'' Lucy said with a sigh.
''He means to elope.''

Her ladyship nearly pricked herself with a pin.
''Elope?''

Resting her head against the bedpost, Lucy murmured, ''He means to elope with Mrs. St. John.''

Lady Philpott threw aside the hat and stood up. She
approached Lucy as though she were a phantasm.
''Do you mean that dreadful harpy? It cannot be
true.''

With an effort, Lucy replied, ''It is true. Mrs. St.
John told me.''

Lady Philpott tottered back to her chair. Seizing a
fan from the dressing table, she waved it violently. She
had been certain that Lucy would fall in love with
Lord Roderick and he with her, so certain, in fact, that
she had gone to the trouble of designing a pretty
curlicued monogram for the future Countess of Silverthorne. This news stunned her as much, nay more,
than the time a link boy had seized her reticule and she
was forced to retrieve it by annointing the lad with her
parasol. She hated to think that Lord Roderick had
taken up with Cora St. John when he might have had
the likes of Lucy Bledsoe. She had thought better of
him. ''Perhaps all is not lost if he takes her only as his
mistress,'' she said in an effort to solace herself.

That idea gave no comfort whatever to Lucy. Nor
did it add to her contentment to hear Lady Philpott
speculate darkly, ''Of course, that vixen will no doubt

snare him for a husband in the end. If she can persuade him to run off with her, she will be able to persuade him to any enormity. There is no stratagem to which some females will not stoop in the hunt for a husband.''

''It is not Mrs. St. John's conduct that troubles me,'' Lucy said, her emotion rising. ''It is Lord Roderick's. I hoped he might consider the lady's reputation, even if she did not. I hoped he might be above taking advantage of a lady in such a position of dependence. I hoped he would know that when he tires of her, he will be welcomed into Society, while she will always be an outcast.''

Lady Philpott could spare no sympathy for Cora St. John. This elopement business was a decided setback. Lucy would never be persuaded to look favourably on a gentleman who had swoofed off with another female. Miss Bledsoe was known to be somewhat strict in her thinking along those lines, and to say the truth, Lady Philpott could not blame her. A husband ought to wait until after the marriage to take a mistress. Not knowing what else to say, she ventured, ''Let us hope this foolish business is merely the St. John creature's doing.''

''But how can that be?'' Lucy cried with such emotion that Lady Philpott was startled. ''After all, she does not mean to bind Lord Roderick and carry him off against his will. I am forced to conclude that he finds the idea much to his liking.'' Here she pressed her lips together as though she had just drunk a bitter draught.

Lady Philpott was also forced to swallow this distasteful logic. She could not imagine any rational gentleman finding the idea of an elopement with Mrs.

St. John to his liking, but she had no illusion as to the odd humours which incited the generality of males: namely, comfort, convenience and folly. Accordingly she shook her head and advised sagely, "You must not attempt to understand the preferences of the male species. It will only confound you. Lord Roderick is certainly very rich and very handsome, but if he truly prefers Cora St. John, I have no opinion of him. I can only wish him joy of her."

In contrast to her ladyship, Lucy could not wish Roderick joy. She could hardly tell what she wished him, for her mind was racing with ideas. In turn, she dwelt on Mrs. St John's difficulty, Lord Roderick's perfidy, the lady's willful self-destruction, the gentleman's unconcern, the former's lack of family and friends, the latter's utter lack of scruples. "One does not expect a man like Turcott to behave like a gentleman," she said miserably, "but Lord Roderick ought to know better. I felt certain, as I came to know him these past days, that he did know better."

"Well, we always hope that others will know better, but they never do. We must resign ourselves to that fact, dear girl, and think of the future." Then, taking her own excellent advice, her ladyship set her mind to thinking about the future in regard to Lucy. If Lord Roderick had taken himself out of the running by saddling himself with a lame mare, then it was high time she set about looking for another stallion to put her money on, metaphorically speaking.

Urgently, Lucy drew near her ladyship. "Then you agree with me, Lady Philpott. You agree that the situation is desperate, that being a widow with no family, Mrs. St. John is in need of help, for she has no one to advise her properly."

In a soothing voice Lady Philpott cooed, "Yes, yes. It is all excessively pitiful. But we must not despair. We must gather our wits and be practical. It is true we have spent nearly a fortnight at Lever Combe to no avail. But we shall leave this house as soon as our trunks can be packed and find a more promising venue. I promise you, we shall unearth an eligible gentleman before September is out. Hampshire is not entirely devoid of male society, I am told."

Aghast, Lucy cried, "What? Leave this house?" The thought of quitting Lever Combe made her cheeks hot. In the height of her anger against Lord Roderick, in the depths of her despair regarding the elopement, it had never occurred to her to leave. "Why should we be in such a hurry?" she asked breathlessly. "We have not stayed our fortnight quite yet."

With a steady hand, Lady Philpott pinned the red feather to the bonnet, saying, "If we are to find the gentleman who is to mend your broken heart, it must be soon. You are not growing any younger, dear girl, and at your time of life you can ill afford to waste time teaching lessons to scoundrels who haven't the taste or morals to learn them."

Lucy put her hands to her face. Her arguments, she realized, had been too strong. Even Lady Philpott, who had been Lord Roderick's firmest ally, was now turned against him. With a spot of colour in her cheeks, she retreated a little, observing, "I do not believe that Lord Roderick is wholly incapable of learning a lesson."

Lady Philpott gave her the fisheye. "My dear girl, did you not just tell me that he is on the point of eloping? Clearly the case is worse than hopeless."

The pink cheeks grew vermillion. "Yes, but I do not think him a complete villain. Indeed, I know him to be capable of the most rational and unselfish conduct."

Lady Philpott stabbed another pin into the bonnet. "What good is that to us?"

"A great deal of good, because, you see, when I pointed out to him that Mr. Hunt bore a tender affection for Miss Crowther-Biggs, Lord Roderick did everything possible to further the match. It seems to me that if he was willing to heed me in that instance, he might do the same in this." Lucy pressed her hands together tensely.

Baffled, her ladyship enquired, "Why go to the trouble, dear girl?"

As pale now as she had been red before, Lucy said, "If I have the courage to be bold, I may be able to persuade Lord Roderick not to elope."

Lady Philpott spat out the pin she held in her lips. Her mouth flapped a moment before she declared she could not believe her ears. What made Lucy think, she asked shrilly, that an unmarried gentleman could be persuaded to do anything which was neither foolish nor expensive?

Lucy's heart sank at this response. Lady Philpott's practicality seemed to dog her everywhere.

"Miss Bledsoe, I feel obliged to oppose any plan that is a waste of time and labour. We have already wasted too much of both at Lever Combe." Decisively her ladyship took up a new pin.

"I suppose you think," Lucy said bleakly, "that because I was unable to make an iota of difference in Sir Vale's philosophy, in spite of all my efforts, I will have no better luck in Lord Roderick's case."

"Well, I had not thought of it, but now you mention it, that is the only sensible view."

Lucy's voice nearly broke as she said, "No doubt you think Lord Roderick would merely laugh at me as he laughs at everything."

"You have pieced it out quite brilliantly. I could not have done better myself. I am persuaded that we must give over all intentions of reforming Lord Roderick. Thank heaven we did not agree to this ridiculous masquerade for a full month!"

Having hoped that Lady Philpott would argue with her instead of agreeing, Lucy felt profoundly oppressed. She hardly knew what to do or say. She knew only that she could not quit the house before seeing Lord Roderick once more.

For a time, she paced, and as the chamber was not large, she could pace only a few steps before turning and pacing in the other direction. At last, she stopped stock-still as it struck her that Lady Philpott was not going to put forward a single argument she wished to hear. Therefore, she must do it herself.

Coming to the lady, she knelt at her feet, and asked softly, "Did we not promise Lady Roderick to teach her son a lesson? Would it not be dishonourable of us to go back on our word without so much as trying?"

"Pooh. You cannot be expected to keep such a promise under these trying conditions."

"Suppose I were to speak to Lord Roderick with all the rationality and earnestness at my command. Do you think he would hear me with indifference?"

Taking Lucy's hand and patting it affectionately, her ladyship answered, "If he does hear you with indifference, dear girl, then he is either in love with Cora St. John or dead. But in either case, he will not be much use to us. No, my dear, we must put away all thoughts of Lord Roderick and lose no time in swoofing off to Hampshire.''

Lucy stood. With all the resoluteness in her gentle soul, she said, ''Lady Philpott, I am determined to speak with Lord Roderick. I am going to entreat him with all my heart not to elope with Mrs. St. John.''

Her ladyship blinked. Then, with the air of a martyr, she threw up her hands, one hat, a red feather and any number of pins. No matter which way she turned, it seemed, events conspired against her. She had set her heart on matching Lucy with Lord Roderick, but now he was about to run away with a female who was no better than she should be. She had persuaded Lucy to play the part of the earl's Canterbury miss, but it had all come to nothing. She had acknowledged defeat and was ready to give up the scheme, but Lucy was determined to pursue it. Life was nothing but vexation.

Most vexatious of all was this determination of Miss Bledsoe's to speak with the earl. Why should that elegant young lady, whose heart had been shattered by another such scoundrel, exert herself to speak with Lord Roderick? Why should she champion such a harpy as Cora St. John? Why should she argue with either of them when they had no notion of propriety or sense? What did Lucy have to gain by interfering? Her ladyship could not make head or tail of the infernal business.

Unless, of course, Lucy had another interest—a personal interest—in the affair.

At this thought, Lady Philpott regarded her young companion with new eyes. Could it be that Lucy's earnest desire to save Mrs. St. John was, in fact, a desire to save Lord Roderick? Could it be that Lucy could not bear the thought of his swoofing off with Cora St. John? Could it be that Lucy was in love with him and did not yet know it? Could it be that she was, after all, destined to be Countess of Silverthorne?

Her spirits reviving, Lady Philpott watched as Lucy knelt to collect the hat, ribbon and pins. The girl moved with grace and smiled with gentleness. She deserved the very best of husbands, one who would take her to live in a fine house, raise her to a position of nobility and permit her to shop to her heart's content. Lady Philpott was not as certain as she had been that Lord Roderick was that husband, but she was willing to give him one last chance if Lucy loved him. Besides, she would just as soon stay at Lever Combe. There was nothing she detested so much as swoofing about.

TWO EVENINGS LATER, Lucy was surprised to find herself seated next to Lord Roderick at dinner. He appeared amiable as ever, as though his conscience troubled him not at all, and as though absence from his betrothed had made his heart grow only fonder. Evading all questions concerning his business in the north, he addressed to Lucy a word regarding the turtle soup, a word spoken with such a tone of laughter, such a hint of innuendo, and so many references to turtledoves that she could not help laughing. He admired her filmy blue gown, which, he observed appreciatively, exactly matched her eyes. To Lucy, who could not take those eyes from his well-formed face, he hardly seemed like a man on the brink of a scandalous elopement.

At last the time came for the ladies to withdraw. Lord Roderick kissed her palm in full view of everyone and walked to where Lord Knatchbull was offering cigars. Lucy followed after the women, marvelling that a gentleman could contemplate the ruination of a defenceless female and all the while appear as delightful as any hero upon the stage.

THE LIBRARY was richly warm with reds and browns. As the sun shone through the narrow casement, it cast a lattice of shadows across the high bookshelves. Upon entering, Lucy saw his lordship seated in a crimson chair, engrossed in reading.

He rose at the sight of her and, if he was surprised at her entrance, did not betray it. In his usual gallant manner, he gestured towards a chair near his. Regarding her face closely, he observed, "How well you look, my love. Evidently my absence has agreed with you."

When she made no reply, he remarked, "You are supposed to cry out against such a charge, Miss Bledsoe. You are supposed to say that my absence left you desolate. It is highly unflattering to my vanity to have you sit there looking so beauteous and so silent."

She looked at him. "Lord Roderick, are you flirting with me?"

"Really, my love, you can hardly expect me to confess to flirting when I know how much you disapprove of it."

Gently she shook her head. "It is not that I disapprove. It is only that I do not understand how it is done, or why."

"And if you did, you would not wish to flirt with a scoundrel. Am I correct?"

She endeavoured to speak tranquilly as she turned the subject. "Lord Roderick, I have come to speak with you on a very important matter."

Folding his arms, he sat back and appraised her. "My dearest love, if flirting is not a very important matter, I do not know what is."

"I have come to speak with you about Mrs. St. John."

Unperturbed, he nodded. "I daresay you know her situation better than most. You have had the misfortune of witnessing her relations with Turcott."

With a sigh, she replied, "Yes, I know her situation."

"Of course, she cannot marry such a fellow. We do not agree upon very many subjects, but I trust you and I agree upon that."

"Yes."

"And would you also agree that she must get to a place of safety until the fellow can be persuaded to behave like a gentleman and release her?"

"That is what I wished to speak with you about."

"You might as well know, Lucy, I think she ought to go north very soon."

"Yes, I know."

His head snapped up. "You know?"

Unflinchingly, she returned his look. "Mrs. St. John told me everything."

He laughed and shrugged. "Well, so much for secrecy. I hope she does not intend to publish the news in *The Times*. I doubt Turcott reads *The Times*, or reads at all, but he is sure to get wind of the plan once it is advertised."

Lucy could no longer contain the words that filled her heart. Her feelings had brimmed too long not to spill over. "My lord," she urged, "have you considered that by taking her north, you will surely ruin her? Even if Mr. Turcott eventually agrees to give her up, she will be regarded as scandalous and forced to live the life of an outcast."

As he regarded her expression, he felt that no female was so bewitching as Lucy Bledsoe when she was pleading a cause. "Yes, I have considered it," he said. "That is precisely why I did not take her with me when I went north."

"But when she does go north, she will be utterly ruined."

"Well, the north is not the liveliest of venues, I admit, but I never heard of it ruining anybody."

"I do not see how it can help ruining her, if you intend to elope with her."

He sat back, lifting an eyebrow as he regarded her. "*Elope?* I do not recollect saying anything about an elopement."

"It was Mrs. St. John who used that appellation for what you were proposing to do, but I must beg you not to do it."

Lucy was surprised to hear him laugh. Then he rose and walked to a carved table where he poured himself a glass of brandy. After tossing it back, he said, "So this is the purpose of your seeking me out in the midst of my studies. You have come to ask me not to elope with Mrs. St. John, a very natural request, it seems, given that I am engaged to you. But what is to become of poor Cora if I do not chivalrously carry her off?"

Lucy, who had expected him to answer with anger, was amazed to see that he did not resent her interference in the least. She felt encouraged to go on. "I understand Mrs. St. John's difficulty and think perhaps there may be a way out of it.''

He waited expectantly, though from his ironic smile, Lucy guessed that his thoughts were not confined to her reply.

"Instead of eloping with Mrs. St. John, and creating a stir, why not find someone else to take her north?'' she reasoned.

He nodded. "Why not, indeed? Wherever I go, Turcott is sure to follow, for he suspects an elopement, too.''

Again, Lucy took heart from his response. Clearly he had no objection to letting someone else travel with Mrs. St. John. The prospect of a separation from her apparently caused him no alarm whatever. "Perhaps *I* might escort the lady,'' she said.

"You?'' he said with a smile which bordered on laughter.

Colouring, Lucy said, "I am sorry you find the suggestion amusing. I assure you, sir, I should like very much to see Mrs. St. John safely out of the way— out of the way of harm, I mean to say.''

"Doesn't it strike you as amusing that my intended bride wishes to travel with my intended mistress? It is a highly novel notion.''

Determined to overcome his ridicule, she said, "I shall make the offer to Mrs. St. John, and I believe she may be brought to accept.''

With a gleam of mischief, he said, "Mrs. St. John is greatly attached to me. What persuasive arts do you mean to employ?''

"Well, I do not know, precisely. Perhaps I will simply use logic, not arts. I will point out, as you did earlier, that she is less likely to be discovered by Mr.

Turcott if she does not travel with you. If by some chance he should discover her in my company, the appearance will be so innocent as to give him no pretext for harming her.'' When she had done, she looked at him hopefully.

"You are delightful when you are logical. Tell me more."

Conscious of his gaze, she glanced away, saying quickly, "But when I take Mrs. St. John from here, I do not think I shall take her north. No, I do not quite fancy the north. It is unfamiliar country to me. I am better acquainted with Worcestershire."

"Worcestershire is your home, I collect. It cannot be Canterbury, for I know every family in the town and its surroundings. Is your family truly named Bledsoe, or is that the name you use only when you are posing as someone's prospective bride?"

For the third time, his answer surprised her. He was quizzing her. He had forgotten entirely about Mrs. St. John and was teasing her about her home. The realization was more heartening than anything she had known in some while. She permitted herself a small smile as she replied, "My acquaintance there consists of the family of Mr. Edward Farrineau. He is the son of Sir Dalton of Langfield. The Farrineaus are a very old and respectable family, I assure you."

He frowned and demanded, "What is this Edward Farrineau to you?"

Taken aback by his abruptness, she replied, "He is my particular friend."

He dismissed Mr. Farrineau with a gesture. "I will not have Mrs. St. John living under the same roof with a single gentleman. Her reputation is in jeopardy enough, as you so astutely pointed out."

Hastening to reassure him, she said, "You needn't worry. Mr. Farrineau is married and, as a newlywed, may be depended upon to be head over ears in love with his wife."

With a brilliant smile, he replied, "In that case, I think Mr. Farrineau the best fellow in the world."

She glanced at him. "Does that mean we are agreed?"

"Not entirely, I'm afraid. Although your arguments have proved vastly entertaining thus far, there is one puzzle. Whatever could possess you to take an avid interest in Mrs. St. John's concerns?"

It was a question she had asked herself many times. She had not yet constructed a satisfactory answer. She replied evasively, saying "Lady Philpott and I have always intended to leave this house by week's end. It will seem the most natural thing in the world if I invite Mrs. St. John to accompany me to my village. No suspicion could possibly be aroused by such a scheme. I shall be able to do a good turn to a fellow creature with no inconvenience to myself or her ladyship."

"I see. You cannot resist Cora's sweet temper and lively companionship. It is all perfectly clear."

Looking down, she said, "To be truthful, I pity her. Who that knows Mrs. St. John's difficulties can help pitying her?"

He moved so that his face came close to hers. Gravely, he said, "I hope you did not mean to quit Lever Combe without saying a proper farewell to the man you are promised to marry."

She saw his stark look. "I felt certain you would be too occupied with Mrs. St. John to concern yourself with my departure."

"Well, you were wrong."

The baldness of his declaration gave her a pang. Lucy sensed that she was in great danger, not only of feeling more than she wished to feel but also of being taken in. Lord Roderick was skilled in the ways of winning a lady's confidence. There was nothing she wanted so much at this moment as to give him hers. But she did not dare.

In a trembling voice, she said, "Lord Roderick, if this is more flirting, I must beg you to go no further. There are circumstances of my past—events which happened only too recently—that make it impossible for me to engage in the sort of easy repartee you find amusing."

"What events, Lucy?" The way he looked at her caused her to think she ought to have kept silent. His expression was disturbingly soft.

Uneasy, she rose and moved to the other side of her chair so that it stood between them. "I cannot speak of those events. You will excuse me, I hope. We were speaking of Mrs. St. John."

"Ah, yes," he said. "It seems we can never stick to the subject of poor Cora."

He had come round the chair and now stood so near that she was tempted to back away. She held her ground, however. "If you have any doubts about my being able to look after her properly, my lord, you may ask the opinion of Lady Philpott."

He paused, then said, "Lady Philpott will vouch for you, will she? Well, I do not know. She is not what one would call disinterested, is she? She knows all about this masquerade you are conducting and will not tell me a thing, a fact which counts heavily against her."

Fascinated by his mischievous smile, Lucy was unable to rise to her ladyship's defence.

"But there is one point in her favour," he said amiably. "I expect she is rather in love with me, and that, in my view, eradicates all her other defects." Fixing her with eyes that seemed to see through her, he added, "I cannot help but admire a lady who is in love with me."

CHAPTER EIGHT

A Surprise

HER CURIOSITY ROUSED, Lady Philpott came to the library at once in response to his lordship's note. As she entered the cavernous room, she had the sense that her words would boom out an echo when she spoke. But there was little danger of that, for she found herself surprised into silence at the sight of Lucy, sitting in a chair near Lord Roderick, engrossed in close, quiet conversation. So intimate did they appear that for a moment the lady thought they had in truth become engaged. Her ladyship instantly concluded that Lucy was once more on civil terms with Lord Roderick and that the gentleman might well be the man of juice she had always thought him.

The earl rose to greet her ladyship, led her to his chair and drew up another for himself.

After looking from Lucy's glowing eyes to Roderick's captivating smile, Lady Philpott waited to hear the reason for her summons. The earl explained the case succinctly: to wit, that he and Miss Bledsoe wished to see Mrs. St. John rescued from Mr. Turcott but that they could not decide on the means. Lady Philpott, whose most recent information regarding Mrs. St. John was that Lord Roderick intended to elope with her, was beside herself with rapture. The earl was instantly restored to her good graces and Mrs. St. John was suddenly greatly to be pitied.

Lucy said to her ladyship, "I should like to take Mrs. St. John with me into Worchestershire. Edward and Susanna Farrineau would surely receive us both. By this means, I shall be able to help Mrs. St. John in a manner that will not bring down scandal upon her head—or Lord Roderick's. But do you think," Lucy enquired, "that I am the proper one to take her?"

"Of course, my dear girl! I cannot say that you have led armies in the manner of Joan of Arc, who was dreadfully forward for a young lady, in my view, but I do believe you are fully capable of enduring a drive to Worcestshire in the company of Mrs. St. John."

"I am glad you think so highly of my qualifications," said Lucy with a smile.

"But," said her ladyship slyly, "should not Lord Roderick accompany you—by way of protection, I mean? The roads abound with highwaymen and the like."

Perceiving her intention, he laughed. "I should like nothing better than to act as your protector and defender, but my comings and goings are far too likely to put Turcott on the scent."

"Oh," said her ladyship, disappointed.

"Moreover, I must visit a certain lady, a lady who on no account can be put off."

This reason pleased Lady Philpott even less than the first. She began to think once more that they would have to give over any idea of snaring the earl. But because Lucy was in love with him, she felt obliged to tolerate his propensity to swoof about from female to female.

Lucy, sinking at the news that his lordship had yet another lady to pay his addresses to, remained painfully silent.

The first to recover was Lady Philpott. She immediately sought a means of getting the earl away from the lady who could not be put off and into Worcestershire as soon as possible. "I shall accompany the ladies on the journey," she declared. "I shall ask Lord Knatchbull to send a number of his servants with us. Then, my lord, you must come to Worcestershire after a week and tell us how we are to dispose of Mrs. St. John."

He tried to win a glance from Lucy but with little success. "I should like to visit Worcestershire," he said, "if my bride has no objection."

In answer to this hint, Lucy only managed to say, "I am certain Mrs. St. John would be pleased to see you." She could not help wondering who this lady was that he had promised to visit and whether she was very beautiful.

"Ah, yes, I keep forgetting poor Cora," he said.

"That is what comes of having so many ladies to think of," her ladyship shot at him.

"I cannot deny it," he said with a smile. "I think a great deal of the ladies."

"But you will not bring any of them with you to Worcestershire, I hope," said Lady Philpott. "You must travel alone—and incognito. From what you say, if your identity were to become known, you might lead Turcott directly to us."

"Precisely," the earl agreed, "and there is nothing so amusing as taking on a false identity and pretending to be what one is not. Is that not true, Miss Bledsoe?"

When Lucy blushéd, he bowed and walked to the door. Then, as though an afterthought had suddenly stuck him, he turned and said, ''By the by, Lucy, I never had any intention of eloping with Cora St. John, in spite of her intention of eloping with me. My plan was always to send her north, not to take her there. However, I do thank you for saving me the trouble of hunting for a means to execute my plan. Whether the lady will thank you is another matter altogether.''

On that, he blew her a kiss and made his exit. Lucy would have felt the full force of self-reproach at this astonishing news if she had not felt such pleasure.

ALTHOUGH THERE WAS MUCH to discuss in the planning of the rescue, especially if they were to set forth the next morning, Lord Roderick found no opportunity of being alone with Lucy the next day. When he suggested a ride to view the ruin of a Roman gate, the other guests got wind of the proposed excursion and clamoured to see the pile of stone left by Caesar's soldiers. Consequently, Roderick was forced to issue a general invitation.

Following their return, Lord Roderick thought he might find Lucy in the library, but when he attempted to leave his chamber in search of her, he was intercepted, first by Mrs. Crowther-Biggs, who scolded him at great length for breaking her heart, and then by Miranda Crowther-Biggs, who apologized at great length for breaking his. By the time he made his escape to the library, Lucy was gone.

When she left the library, Lucy went to her bedchamber and endeavoured to be rational. It was becoming clear to her that the motive of revenge which had first brought her to Lever Combe had long since

faded. Her object of teaching Lord Roderick a sound
lesson had been all but forgotten. The earl had made
more conquests among the female sex than anyone she
had heard of in either life or legend, and it was beginning to seem as though she was destined to be one of
them. She could not hear of his intended elopement or
the proposed visit to a mysterious lady without feeling stricken. Nor could she feel his eyes on her without experiencing a glow of consciousness. If he
attended to her and her alone, she feared and doubted;
if he attended to others, she mourned. Her feelings
were a riot of contradiction. It appeared that she had
learned nothing from being crossed in love by Sir Vale.
It was not Lord Roderick who had dire need of lessons; it was Lucy Bledsoe.

AFTER DINNER, in the drawing room, Lord Knatchbull took it into his head to recount to Lucy the tale of
the poacher, whom he claimed to have caught single-
handed. As her host regaled her with the adventure,
Lucy looked towards the earl and found him looking
at her. For a time, it seemed as though he stared at her
absently, perhaps without seeing her. Then, abruptly,
he left the ladies who surrounded him and headed in
Lucy's direction. She observed him and the hard set of
his jaw, wishing she could keep her pulse from
pounding.

The earl interrupted his host in midsentence to say
to him, "Are you aware, my lord, that Mrs. Crowther-
Biggs admires you greatly? Why, she confided the fact
to me this morning, and I thought it might please you
to know it."

This information instantly sent the gentleman off, with smacking lips and lighted eyes, in pursuit of the unsuspecting lady.

Lucy could not help laughing at the ploy, and when Lord Roderick sat, she asked if he had not played an ungrateful trick upon a lady with whom he had lately been on the closest terms of friendship.

"I had to find some way of getting near you. If the fates plot to keep us apart, I must employ heroic measures to bring us together." Here he smiled at her in such a way that it took all her strength to recall that he was on the point of visiting an unnamed lady. Quietly, she asked, "Have you spoken to Mrs. St. John?"

"I have had no opportunity, and at the moment, I am otherwise occupied."

"When will you speak to her? The hour grows late and she must hurry and pack her things if we are to leave in the morning."

"Do not distress yourself, Lucy. I shall speak with her in good time. Just now, I mean to speak with you."

"But in an hour we shall all retire and then you will have lost your chance."

"My plan is to speak to her after we have all retired."

This was almost too much for Lucy. If he meant to speak to the lady after she had retired, then he meant to see her in her chamber. The image of Lord Roderick and Cora St. John together in such a setting was profoundly troubling, as was the knowledge that he would soon trade the widow's boudoir for another's.

"Now, if we have done with poor Cora, I must have a parting word with you, my dear bride. After all, we

shall both set off tomorrow and must appear properly desolate at the prospect."

"A more pressing matter at the moment," she said,
"is what we are to tell Lady Knatchbull. I would not
have it known that I am taking Mrs. St. John into
Worcestershire. Should Turcott enquire, she would tell
him everything."

"We shall give it out that you are going to Canterbury. But, my dearest, if you expect me to keep my
mind on this excellent plan of ours, you must contrive not to look so lovely."

It was with some difficulty that she replied, "Lord
Roderick, before we part, I wish to say that my posing as your betrothed was the most ill-advised and ill-
natured thing I have ever done. I am sorry for it and
hope you will overlook it. Perhaps by assisting Mrs.
St. John, I may salve my conscience a little."

"Is that why you have not told me who you really
are, because your conscience troubles you?"

She met his look and found it full of merriment.

"My dear Miss Bledsoe," he said, "you cannot
possibly have as troubled a conscience as I am blessed
with. Why, I have been guilty of more shameful conduct in a week than any three Englishmen in a lifetime. It is what makes me such an interesting fellow.
If there is any creature who would understand if you
opened your heart to him, it is I."

She smiled. "You are as persuasive as you are compassionate, sir."

"I read philosophy at Oxford."

"Which is why your arguments are so self-serving,
I daresay."

Abruptly, he moved close to her. "You need not tax
your conscience, Lucy. I know nothing about you, but

I do know you are a lady of character. If we were not engaged, I daresay I should be in some danger of losing my heart to you."

His laughter put to rest any alarm she might have felt at this declaration. Moreover, she was grateful to know that he did not think ill of her, in spite of her pose. But unwelcome thoughts would obtrude. She knew that he must soon visit a lady, as he had visited so many ladies, and she knew that he must visit Cora St. John in her chamber, as he had visited so many ladies in their chambers. Consequently, she assumed a reserved air and said, "I trust all will go off as planned." On this, she extracted her hand, rose and went to hear Owen Hunt sing a duet with his lady love.

CORA ST. JOHN was not easily convinced to trade the Earl of Silverthorne for Miss Bledsoe. She stamped her foot and, loudly and tearfully, upbraided Roderick. He sat in a chair, examined the pages of a novel and poked his fingers into her jewellery boxes and rouge pots until she had done ranting. When she finally ran out of breath, he said simply, "Cora, I never said I meant to take you anywhere. You concocted that scheme without consulting me. If you wish to get away from Turcott you will either have to accompany Miss Bledsoe or you will have to find another rescuer."

"It would serve you right if I did go back to Turcott."

"If you wish to wound me, that would be the way to do it."

"Ah, Roddy, you do love me a little, don't you?"

"You know my opinion of love, Cora. It is the means by which the sexes endeavour to get the better of each other."

This reply did not satisfy. Therefore, she pouted. "I do not like this Lucy Bledsoe of yours. It is villainous to force me to travel in her company. Now I shall have to sit and hear her boast of your attentions to her and speak of her wedding clothes. It will gall me beyond bearing to hear it. I shall not be able to withstand such torture."

"It will not be torture, for we are not engaged," he announced as he inspected a hole in one of her kid gloves.

"But she said you were. *You* said you were."

"I lied." He poked a finger through the hole.

"You lied? But why?"

"Boredom, my dear. The truth becomes tedious so quickly, especially during a summer season in the country." He threw the glove aside to smile at her pleasantly.

Delighted, she asked, "Did you really lie? You are not just saying that to make me feel better?"

"I don't know why it should make you feel better to know I am a liar, Cora, but that is what I am. I invented this engagement so that I might flirt with the ladies without ever having to offer them marriage."

She gave him a sidelong glance. "That was very wicked of you, Roddy, but I am glad to hear it."

"You would have every right to be angry with me."

She took a step towards him. "I cannot be angry when you give me such news. And one cannot help liking Miss Bledsoe a little. Now that she is no longer engaged to you, I shall not have to rail at her like a fishwife when she speaks to me."

He leaned forward, saying seriously, "Cora, you must not tell anyone what I have said. This supposed engagement makes Turcott's suspicions about us ap-

pear preposterous. I had better remain promised to
Miss Bledsoe until you reach Worcestershire."

With a shrug, she replied, "Very well, she may
continue the pose."

"And you will go with her?"

Darting him an amorous look, she said, "I would
much rather go with you." Here she came near and
would have sat on his lap if he had not stood before
she reached his chair.

Patiently, he replied, "I have already explained why
we cannot travel together. You shall go with Miss
Bledsoe, and I shall come to you in a week's time.
Then we shall see what else is to be done."

Content to know she would be reunited with him
soon, she presented herself to be kissed, but instead of
availing himself of her cheek, he put her hand to his
lips and went in search of Mr. Hunt.

OWEN DISAPPROVED ENTIRELY. The scheme would
end in disaster, he predicted. While Lord Roderick
lounged on the bed, drinking his friend's brandy,
Owen paced and preached against interfering in another man's engagement, against trusting an imposter, against making love to scores of women at a time
and against doing anything at all save falling in love
and getting married like a proper fellow.

"You have grown tiresome since winning the hand
and heart of the fair Miranda," said his lordship, stifling a yawn. "Now you wish the same fate on me."

"What you call tiresome is merely good sense."

Thoughtfully, the earl set down his glass and rested
his hands behind his head. "Owen, what is your
opinion of Miss Bledsoe?"

"She seems a very elegant young woman, but do not forget she is an imposter. She is after something, Roderick. Be on your guard."

"It was she who gave me the first hint that you were in love with Miss Crowther-Biggs."

"Miss Bledsoe gave you the first hint?"

"In point of fact, she gave me a gentle scolding for not seeing what was plain as a pikestaff to her."

Owen was forced to confess that he had liked her from the first, in spite of himself. "Very well, I agree that Miss Bledsoe is an admirable young woman, and that if she approves of this foolish rescue, then I shall give it my blessing, too. But if you get into a pickle, as I am sure you will, I hope you will know where to find me."

"Worshipping at the altar of Miss Crowther-Biggs, no doubt."

"You may sneer, Roderick, but wait until you are head over ears in love. It will be a different story then."

The earl inspected his fingernails. "I doubt I will be as fortunate as you, Owen, for you have a heart susceptible to Cupid's darts, whereas mine has been hardened from long disuse."

Mr. Hunt sighed and expressed the hope his lordship would not end with a broken head at the hands of that blackguard Turcott.

"You will say nothing about this," Lord Roderick said.

"I will keep mum."

"You will not confide in anyone at all, not even Miss Crowther-Biggs."

Offended, Owen said, "I have already said I will keep mum. And I wish you would not imply that

Miranda is not to be trusted. I am sure if I did say anything to her, she would know how to keep a secret.''

"I am sorry if I implied anything to the contrary, but the situation is dangerous. If anything should happen to Miss Bledsoe, I would blame myself. She is an innocent party in all this, undertaking to protect Cora St. John, who will repay her only with ingratitude. She deserves a knighthood, not a threat upon her life. Do you understand me, Owen?''

Mr. Hunt stared at the earl. Having never before heard him speak of a woman with such admiration, such intensity, such force, the young man now began to understand Lord Roderick very well.

THE FOLLOWING MORNING, under a grey drizzle, the trunks were loaded into the cart, which set off at once. Lady Philpott issued from the front door under an umbrella held aloft by a footman. Outside, she inspected the small army of servants Lord Knatchbull had put at her disposal. Assured that they were all strong, burly and villainous-enough looking to frighten off would-be highwaymen, she nodded her approval. Mrs. St. John came out to join her, as did the ladies' maids. Lord and Lady Knatchbull stepped outside next to wish them all a smooth journey. They all stood huddled against the rain to hear Lady Philpott announce that as Canterbury was not far, they should not experience more than several hours of sickness owing to the swaying and bumping of the carriage.

While these goodbyes were said out of doors, Lord Roderick detained Lucy in the hall for a final word.

"Well, you are off to visit the fortunate Farrineaus," he said. "I wish you a pleasant journey."

"And you are off to visit a lady," she replied quietly, "a lady who on no account can be put off."

He smiled. "I am going to visit my mother. It has been too long since I have seen her."

"Your mother!" she exclaimed, her eyes shining. "How excellent of you to think of visiting your mother. I cannot tell you how happy I am to hear it." Her smile was full and warm.

He raised an eyebrow. "If I had had any idea you were so fond of filial visits, I should have made one sooner."

Lowering her eyes, she said, "I don't believe I mentioned that I am acquainted with your mother."

"Are you, indeed? No, you did not mention it, as you know very well."

After meeting his look and seeing that he waited for more, she added, "You must ask her to tell you all about our engagement."

This hint amused him. Moving close to her, he said softly, "I am well aware that when a man has questions, he can do no better thing than to consult his mother." He lifted her chin with his fingers.

Conscious of his sweet breath, she closed her eyes. She opened them again when the door suddenly flew wide and the footman announced that the carriage was ready. The servant stood ramrod-straight against the doorpost, prepared to open an umbrella as soon as the earl and the young lady should exit. The others, still standing in the grey mist, looked at them expectantly.

Lord Roderick bowed dramatically to them and then to Lucy. "I take leave of my betrothed now," he announced to one and all, and to their amazement, he kissed her hard and long upon her parted lips.

The instant he took her in his arms, a familiar sensation captured Lucy, the sensation of being swept along. Whispers in the ear became one with urgent caresses on her back and a far-off sense that she shivered. She scarcely knew that she held Roderick's face, or that she pressed herself to him, or that she sought his lips. Indeed, she scarcely hardly knew how, minutes later, she came to be installed in the carriage, or when the horses had been shouted forward, or why Lady Philpott sighed and simpered over her so contentedly.

CHAPTER NINE

Revelations

"I KNOW ALL ABOUT the pretence," Cora St. John announced when they had been riding for upwards of an hour.

Lucy stared at the distant hills, pale green in the rain. She was too rapt in the recollection of what had passed in the hall at Lever Combe and too lulled by the rocking of the coach to attend to conversation.

"That is why he kissed you," Cora said, "merely for the sake of the pretence."

Lady Philpott glared at the woman. "I do not know why Lord Roderick should kiss anybody unless he wanted to."

Cora smirked. "He has told me the entire tale. I know that he is not in reality engaged."

Lucy heard enough now to rouse her from her pleasant musings. The glow which had warmed her since the departure from the house began to dissipate. Gazing out the window, she saw that the silver drizzle had turned to slashing rain.

Lady Philpott was not disposed to believe a word of what dropped from the lips of Cora St. John, who had tried to gammon Miss Bledsoe with a wholly fictitious story about an elopement. She only hoped that Lucy would not be taken in. The dear girl was inexperienced in the ways of the world. Moreover, being crossed in love had rendered her tender on the subject of men. Whatever was damaging to their character inflamed that tenderness all the more. Her ladyship suspected that Lord Roderick's character could not withstand much more of a damaging nature without seriously affecting Miss Bledsoe's heart. At the first opportunity, she would warn her young companion not to credit anything said by Cora St. John.

It struck Lucy that beneath her rouge and black feathers, Cora St. John was a remarkably handsome woman. It did not surprise her in the least that Lord Roderick admired her. "You have known Lord Roderick a long time," she said.

"I've known him forever," Cora answered. "He warned me against engaging myself to Turcott, but as he refused to marry me himself, I did not have any choice. A woman must marry someone, you know."

This last observation, Lady Philpott thought, was the first sensible word Mrs. St. John had uttered in her earshot.

"It appears Lord Roderick was right in his estimation of Mr. Turcott," Lucy observed.

"Yes, and he would have fought a duel on my account if I had asked him to."

Lucy could not remain entirely composed as she replied, "It is highly unusual for a woman's lover to defend her honour against her betrothed. I believe the reverse is generally the case."

"I suppose it does look odd. That must be why Roderick declined to shoot Turcott but urged me to break with him instead. Unfortunately, it is Roddy who is in danger of being killed. Turcott is dreadfully jealous."

Glancing once more at the bleak weather, Lucy replied, "Lord Roderick is many things I disapprove of, but I should not like to see him shot."

"Nor I, which is why I think it clever of him to have kissed you as he did."

Lady Philpott stated firmly, "I'm sure he did not do it to be clever."

"Oh, but he did!" Cora contradicted. "He knew it would put Turcott off the scent. If he questions anyone at Lever Combe, he will hear that Lord Roderick is in love with his Canterbury bride, was even seen to kiss her in full view of everyone. There will be no suspicion of Roddy's violent attachment to me."

Lucy considered this painful view of the matter. His lordship's kiss had not felt like pretence or cleverness or anything of the sort. Yet she must acknowledge that he was what he was. He had known scores of women and was no doubt greatly skilled in giving an appearance of sincerity. In the case of such a man, it was impossible to know what his kisses truly meant. The only way to find out was to see him again, and that event would not take place for another week, a very long week.

Two minutes after his arrival at Queenscroft, Lord Roderick sat his mother down on a brocaded sofa and asked her what she knew of Lucy Bledsoe.

Lady Roderick, who at the appearance of her son had instantly forgotten her quarrel with him, said sheepishly, "Oh, dear."

He walked to the mantelpiece and turned to face her, smiling. His scarlet coat and velvet collar set off his dark hair, so that his mother could not blame the women for finding him devilishly handsome.

"You need not be alarmed," he said. "I have no complaint to make of the young lady. I only wish to know why she pretends to be engaged to me and what the deuce you have to do with it."

"Oh, Roderick." She put her hand to her unfashionably powdered hair. "You will think I have been very wicked."

"That will be a pleasant change. Usually it is you who think that I have been very wicked, and not without cause."

"What did she tell you?"

"Only that I ought to speak to you about my engagement. I gather from what little she said that you know about the scheme. Now tell me everything. I've been patient long enough, and I require answers."

Lady Roderick smoothed the folds of her purple dress, saying tearfully, "Miss Bledsoe undertook the pose because I asked her to. It was very bad of me, I know, but you have no one to blame but yourself—giving it out that I was the cause of your loveless engagement to some girl in Canterbury, who did not even exist. Why, you made me out to be the horridest creature. For shame."

Laughing, he went to his mother, knelt and took her hand in both of his. "Do you mean to say that you conceived this idea of bringing my betrothed to life? I had not thought you capable of such a humbug, though a very amusing one it is."

She brought his hand to her soft, rouged cheek. "I did not conceive the idea. I only wish I had. It was Miss Bledsoe who thought of it."

He rose and looked down at her. "But why? Did I harm her or her family in some manner?"

"She wished to teach you a lesson."

This scarcely cleared up the mystery. "Why should Miss Bledsoe wish to teach me a lesson? She had never met me in her life. I'm certain I would have remembered meeting her if I had. I could forget, indeed I *have* forgotten, a great many women, but I could not forget Miss Bledsoe."

"No, you had never met her, Roderick. But not long ago, she met a man much like yourself. She was thinking of him, not you, when the scheme occurred to her."

This piece of news gave him pause. Gravely he asked, "What has such a fellow to do with me?"

"You both go about breaking women's hearts. Therefore she concluded that you were a scoundrel, like the gentleman she loved."

He scowled at the clock on the mantel. "She was in love with him?"

"Lady Philpott says so, and I believe poor Lucy was very much in love, for she feels things deeply, you know."

"Yes, I know."

"And you must admit, Roderick, you have behaved so badly at times that you might easily be mistaken for a scoundrel."

He frowned, not amused in the least to be compared to a man Lucy despised, nor pleased in the least to know that Lucy had not long ago been in love. "Well," he said, "so Miss Bledsoe's heart has been broken. That explains a great deal."

"Lucy did not wish to pose as she did. Indeed, she was sure she could not pull it off—she does not lie as easily as a young lady ought to do. But if you say you have learned your lesson and will not tell any more vile tales about your mother, then you need not be engaged to Miss Bledsoe any longer, and I shall be content."

Restless, he paced. "You may be content, but I am not. I am afraid I like Miss Bledsoe a good deal better than I thought I would like a prospective bride."

When Lady Roderick absorbed this statement, she regarded him in dismay, then in horror. Standing, she cried, "You like her? Oh, never say so!"

"You ought to approve, Mother. If you like her, why shouldn't I?"

Grasping him by the arm, she said, "Heaven help the female you like, Roderick. I forbid you to like Miss Bledsoe! You will break her heart, just as the other one did, and I shall never forgive myself—or you, either."

At this dire warning, he laughed. "So you, too, think I am a scoundrel. It must be your mother's partiality that sees me in such an heroic light."

"I never said you were a scoundrel, dear boy. It is only that you are in the habit of making love to women whom you do not intend to marry. Miss Bledsoe is not the sort of young lady who indulges in such flirtations. She is the sort who is courted by a gentleman and then, after a decent time, dressed in wedding clothes and carried to the altar in proper form."

Smiling, he chided her. "You know my opinion of marriage, Mother. I cannot possibly consider it for another fifty or sixty years."

"I am aware of that, and so I beg you to spare Miss Bledsoe, for I am sure that if you were to be charming to her, she would not be able to help falling in love with you."

"You may rest assured, Miss Bledsoe has contrived to find me highly resistable."

Lady Roderick did not believe it. "If she has contrived to hold out against you, it is only because she is superior to most others in her mind and character. But she cannot do so forever."

"I am delighted to hear you say so. You are apparently of the opinion that she must submit to my manifold charms at last."

"Be serious, Roddy," she begged. "And please do not see her again. Only your absence can keep her safe."

Vastly entertained by such a notion, he said, "I mean to see her in a week's time."

"Mercy on us all. I wish you would not."

"I must. I have promised to meet her in Worcestershire."

"Break your promise. Be charitable."

He grew serious. "I cannot do that."

"But what will you do when you arrive in Worcestershire? Will you make love to her and break her heart all over again? Even you could not be so cruel."

It astonished him to think that his desire to see Lucy could be misconstrued as cruelty—and by his own mother. "I shall do as I always do," he said. "That is to say, I shall do exactly as I please," and as his mother answered his declaration with a piteous groan, he planted a kiss on her forehead and hied himself off to the stables.

IN SPITE OF the violence of their passion, Owen Hunt and Miss Crowther-Biggs felt uncommonly dull. The past two days had taken nearly all the guests from Lever Combe. Another party of visitors was not expected for some days. How to fill the interim in an amusing fashion was a difficulty, until Mr. Hunt hit upon the strategy of making interesting conversation. He had tried a dozen or so subjects and failed miserably with each one until he happened to mention Miss Bledsoe, a name which provoked a woeful sigh in his beloved.

"I did what I could to save the earl from Miss Bledsoe," Miranda whispered to Owen as they strolled arm in arm along the lyme walk. "It took all my courage, and discovery would have sullied my reputation, but I did try to save him."

Puzzled, he asked, "What do you mean?"

"When I first learned of his engagement, I wrote to his mother, begging her to set him free from bondage to a young lady he abhorred. And now that you and I are to be married and to live happily ever after, I am even more appalled at Lord Roderick's fate. I wish his mother were not so hard-hearted."

It took Owen some time to comprehend the fact that Miranda had written to Lady Roderick in regard to her son's engagement, but when at last the idea penetrated, he could not help laughing.

Vexed, she said, "Do you laugh at the earl's misfortune?"

"I am not laughing at *him*, my dearest one."

"Then you are laughing at me," she concluded tearfully.

Containing his mirth, he soothed her. "I have news that will comfort you, my sweetest love. You will not have to pity his lordship a moment longer. Your gentle heart may rest at ease, for Roderick is not engaged at all. He and Miss Bledsoe were merely pretending."

The tears vanished; Miranda gazed at him through narrowed eyes. "He is not engaged?"

"He never was! It was all a ruse to fend off amorous females. Poor Roderick is beset by ladies young and old wishing to snare him. So he invented a young lady in Canterbury."

Her lips thinning, she said, "You were right, Owen. I no longer feel sorry for Lord Roderick."

"I am glad to have put your worries to rest."

"We must go into the house now. I must find Mother."

"But we have only begun our walk."

"Bother our walk! I must tell Mama what you have told me. She will be very interested to know of Lord Roderick's charade."

"Oh, you must not tell her. Indeed, I ought not to have told you. It is a secret."

"But I must tell Mama. You see, I believe she nurtures something of a tendre for the gentleman. This happy news must dispel that unfortunate attachment. In fact, I should not be surprised if Mama were furious and looked for a way to punish the wicked scoundrel."

ALTHOUGH EDENHURST had been built in the last century, it was constructed after the Jacobean style. Built of blood-red brick, it had been renovated by Mr. Marlowe years before and furnished with such lavish ostentation that it had become something of a joke in the neighbourhood of Cheedham. During the years when Mr. Marlowe had lived in the West Indies, the house had failed to find a buyer, despite its situation on rising ground and its spacious deer park. It had stood empty long enough to require a complete renovation upon his return. With the advice of his daughter Susanna and his son-in-law Edward, Mr. Marlowe had restrained his taste for show. Thus, Edenhurst had been fashioned into one of the finest houses of the county.

Hearing a carriage, Susanna Farrineau ran into the circular drive. The instant the servant handed out her old friend Lucy Bledsoe, she threw her arms about her neck. She then greeted Lady Philpott warmly, welcomed Mrs. St. John graciously and apologized repeatedly for the absence of her father and husband. "Papa and Edward never would have gone into Cheedham if they had known you were going to surprise us."

"I hope you do not mind our coming," Lucy said. "We were in too great a hurry to write you of our plans."

The ladies went inside the house, where they refreshed themselves with tea and cakes. Susanna looked at them all with great curiosity, especially Mrs. St. John, who was a stranger, waiting impatiently for some explanation of the sudden visit. She was forced to wait a considerable time, which excited her curiosity all the more. At last Lady Philpott had eaten and drunk her fill and asked to have the housekeeper show her to a bedchamber so that she might rest. Soon Cora St. John did likewise, leaving the two young women to themselves.

As soon as Lucy had supplied the details of the rescue, Susanna clapped her hands together, enthralled. "It is a remarkable adventure. Why, you might have been followed by the villainous Mr. Turcott and had your head blown to pieces."

Lucy smiled. "That is scarcely my idea of an adventure."

Clapping her hand to her mouth, Susanna frowned. "I must not say such things any more. I have promised Edward that I shall speak and behave like a lady, and I mean to keep my word."

With a squeeze of the hand, Lucy replied, "I hope you will always be exactly what you are, which is the dearest creature in all the world."

"That is what Edward says, though he is my husband and is obliged to say agreeable things to me. I only wish there were such a man for you."

Shaking her head, Lucy replied softly, "I shall have to be blessed with your good sense, Susanna, before I can be blessed with such a husband as Mr. Farrineau."

The plaintive note under these words did not escape Susanna. "If you regard me as having good sense," she said, "then you must be in great difficulty."

Lucy confessed with a sigh that she was in very great difficulty indeed.

"You are not still in love with Sir Vale Saunders!" Susanna exclaimed.

Hardly knowing whether to laugh or to cry, Lucy answered, "I would have to be a fool to love such a man, wouldn't I?"

Vehemently, Susanna nodded agreement. "Worse than a fool."

The way Lucy looked at her then, with her eyes full and her lips smiling wistfully, told Susanna much that was left unsaid. "I ought not to have called you a fool," Susanna mourned. "Oh, will I never learn to curb my tongue!"

"You will be glad to know that the gentleman in question is not Sir Vale. However, you will not be glad to know that he resembles Sir Vale in a number of ways, the very worst of ways. He comes to us soon, so that we may decide what is to be done with Mrs. St. John. You will see him then.''

Susanna said, ''I conclude it is Lord Roderick you are speaking of, the gentleman who has befriended your unfortunate companion. But he does not sound so very bad to me. He has, from what you tell me, done a brave thing for Mrs. St. John. Are you quite sure he is as bad as Sir Vale?''

''I'm afraid he will end by taking Mrs. St. John to the Continent, which will be construed as an elopement.''

''Nonsense. From what you tell me, that is what he most wishes to avoid.''

Thanks to the lengthy carriage ride with the talkative widow, Lucy had resigned herself once more to the idea of an elopement, so that she was able to say with some appearance of calm, ''Mrs. St. John means to persuade him otherwise, and I should not be surprised if she were to succeed, for the Earl of Silverthorne enjoys nothing so much as being a great favourite with the ladies. I do not know what is to be done with her if he does not take her away.''

Susanna refused to be downcast. ''We shall think of something else to do with the woman. I have one or two notions, but I daresay they might shock you, as well they should, for they are perfectly shocking, and not at all the sort of thing you would agree to, for you are far too elegant to abandon a lady you have gone to all the bother of rescuing, no matter how inconvenient she proves to be.''

Here Lucy laughed. ''How very refreshing it is to see you, Susanna. You are a tonic.''

''I daresay, Edward will know how to dispose of Mrs. St. John. He always knows what is best. And in a few days, I shall have a look at this Lord Roderick of yours and tell you what I think, though I am sure, even without having set eyes on him, that he is not half good enough for you."

LADY KNATCHBULL was overseeing four tables of card players when a commotion was heard outside the saloon. Turcott noisily pushed his way past a footman and came inside. As usual, his presence infused the air with the stink of horses, ale and tobacco. Without greeting his hostess, the man stalked to each of the tables in turn in order to inspect the faces of the players. His scrutiny completed, he demanded of Lady Knatchbull, "What have you done with Mrs. St. John?"

Her ladyship was obliged to answer, if only for the sake of the guests who gawked at the intruder, "We no longer have the pleasure of entertaining Mrs. St. John at Lever Combe."

"Pleasure, my arse," he snarled. "You're hiding her, I warrant. You wish to deprive a gentleman of his rights."

"We should like to return to our piquet, with your permission," answered her ladyship. "I assure you, the lady has left this house."

He treated her to an ugly stare. "Well, where has she gone to then? Where has that blackguard taken her?"

Mrs. Crowther-Biggs and Miranda, who sat opposite each other at one of the tables, exchanged a significant glance. Each nodded to the other. Then, before Lady Knatchbull could respond to Turcott's question, the two ladies approached, the mother stating grandly, "If we may speak with you privately, sir, we shall give you all the information you crave."

With a grateful sigh, Lady Knatchbull led the three to an anteroom off the saloon. As soon as the servant shut the door, leaving them alone, the ladies faced Turcott, who regarded them contemptuously. "There is something we have to tell you," said the mother.

"I will do the talking," he said impatiently. "You will answer me when I tell you to and not before. Now, tell me where he has taken her."

Miranda raised her chin high to say, "If I were you, I should listen to what my mother has to say. I believe it will interest you greatly."

"Quiet!" he demanded, offending her into silence.

"Mrs. St. John is travelling with Miss Bledsoe and Lady Philpott," said Mrs. Crowther-Biggs.

"You are a liar!" he replied.

She flared, "You clot! You do not know the truth when you hear it."

Shaking his head, he said, "You cannot hoodwink me. She has gone off with Roderick."

Miranda and her mother looked at one another. Evidently, there was no reasoning with the man. He would not be helped.

Seizing Mrs. Crowther-Biggs by the arm, he warned that he would break her in half if she did not tell him all. She tore herself from his grasp in a fury. Then, adjusting her person, she said, "You say you wish to know where they have gone? Well, they have gone to Canterbury. That is where they have gone!"

"Aha!" he cried. "To Roderick's estate, no doubt!"

"Miss Bledsoe lives in Canterbury," said the young Miss Crowther-Biggs. She had grown very red-cheeked in the past minutes; her mother had grown quite pale beneath her rouge.

Puzzled, Turcott repeated, "You say that Miss Bledsoe has taken Cora to her house in Canterbury? But why?"

Mrs. Crowther-Biggs did not condescend to answer. This Mr. Turcott had repaid her kind offer to help with insults. She began to think better of her intention to give him information. Indeed, of the two men who had lately offended her, she found Turcott the more unforgivable at the moment.

Shaking his head in disbelief, Turcott said, "I may be in my cups, but I warrant I am clear-headed enough to know that a man's bride is not likely to aid and abet him in an elopement with his mistress. What the devil can it mean?" He looked at the two ladies for an answer.

They looked at each other. Miranda waited to see if her mother would reveal that no engagement did in fact exist. Mrs. Crowther-Biggs waited to see if her daughter would speak. To their mutual surprise, both kept mum.

Turcott rubbed his temple, then declared, "I have no more business with the likes of you," and went out.

When she was sure he was gone, Miranda cried, "Oh, Mama, I thought you were going to tell him the truth."

"I thought *you* were," Mrs. Crowther-Biggs said with a sigh.

The two women remained thoughtful for a time. As there was nothing else to do, they went to rejoin the others in the saloon. Before they entered, however, Mrs. Crowther-Biggs stopped her daughter to say, "You will think me foolish, but I am not sorry to have said nothing. Roderick deserves his comeuppance, I'm sure, but I haven't the heart to give it to him."

Patting her mother's hand, Miranda confessed, "I am equally foolish, Mama, for I am glad we were silent, and though it shames me to say so, if Turcott does murder Lord Roderick, I shall bring flowers to his grave."

TWO DAYS AFTER Lord Roderick had left Queenscroft, Lady Roderick received a visitor. The gentleman, who claimed to be acquainted with her son, shocked her by his appearance, which was dirty and slovenly, by his air, which was ill-mannered and rough, and by his aroma, which was disgusting to a lady accustomed to sprinkling dried rose petals throughout her rooms. "What is it you want?" she enquired.

Bowing and gesturing wide with his hat, Turcott said, "I come calling on his lordship, if you please."

"Lord Roderick is not here, as the servant must have informed you."

"Can you tell me where he has gone to?"

"What is your business with him?"

"I have been seeking Miss Bledsoe these several days and nights. I am told her family live in Canterbury, but it appears no one has ever heard of them."

Lady Roderick grew uneasy and knew not how to reply.

"I thought perhaps Lord Roderick would tell me where to find her, being engaged to her and that."

Her ladyship's uneasiness increased tenfold. She had not anticipated that her little joke on her son would require her to lie to all the world. Indeed, she had no intention of lying to another soul now that she had unfolded the truth to Roderick. "Oh, they are not engaged!" she said. "It was only a hum. You must pay it no mind."

Turcott's red face grew redder, but he kept his countenance, saying only, "Miss Bledsoe has done me the honour of assisting the woman I am to marry. I owe her a great debt, and I'm a man who pays his debts. That's why I wish to find her, to pay her what she is owed."

Hearing this explanation, her ladyship softened towards the man. "Miss Bledsoe has gone to Worcestershire, sir, to the village of Cheedham. You may enquire after her there."

Without thanking her, Turcott took his leave, while Lady Roderick smiled to think that there were some honest folk left in the world who, though coarse and unwashed, were not afraid to go to the trouble of repaying a debt.

CHAPTER TEN

Reversals

AFTER DINNER, as the household gathered in the sumptuous red saloon, Mrs. St. John's history was unfolded to Edward Farrineau and Susanna's father, Mr. Marlowe. Both gentlemen would have expressed their shock and concern to the lady, but she prevented any displays of kindness by avoiding their company and that of everyone at Edenhurst. Whenever Lucy came upon Cora St. John in the corridors or the stairway, the woman fled her presence. Mrs. St. John declined to walk out of doors, even though the park was inviting and tame deer frequently came there to be fed by hand.

One morning, when Lucy and Mrs. St. John both happened to enter the gallery at the same time, Lucy seized the opportunity to say, "I regret that you are not pleased with Edenhurst. It will not be long before his lordship arrives and finds a more suitable place for you."

"Edenhurst is very well," said the lady impassively.

Both stared awkwardly at an enormous portrait of a military gentleman who had no connection with the Marlowes but whose likeness had been among the accoutrements of the house.

"Did you hear a noise last night?" Mrs. St. John
asked. "I thought I heard footsteps."

"I heard nothing." Then, after a pause, Lucy added
gently, "If you are frightened, I shall ask Mr. Marlowe to post one or two servants about the grounds."

Mrs. St. John bit her lip. "Yes, do tell him to post
two servants." She gave another look at the grim
gentleman who loomed over the gallery. Then, without a word, she returned to her chamber nearly at a
run.

Lucy deduced from this meagre conversation that
Mrs. St. John feared discovery by Mr. Turcott and
indeed was anxious enough to keep indoors. She did
not know Cora St. John well, but she knew her enough
to assume that the woman would not confess her fears,
especially not to her. Therefore, Lucy contented herself with speaking to Mr. Marlowe as promised.

The good man lost no time in appointing two of his
most trusted hands to patrol the park and the lanes.
Only one day later, the men reported that two ugly-
looking ruffians had been seen dawdling on the path
between Edenhurst and the village. When Mr. Marlowe's men asked about the fellows in the village, they
were told that the men had been enquiring about Miss
Bledsoe and her travelling companions.

As soon as he received this alarming report, Mr.
Marlowe whispered it to Lucy, who thought it best to
keep the information to herself until such time as she
could communicate it to Lord Roderick. There was no
profit in further distressing Mrs. St. John. Lucy herself was not a little uneasy, and could not help thinking of the most dreadful possibilities. What would
happen, she wondered, if Turcott actually presented
himself at Edenhurst? What would happen if he did so

before the earl's arrival? What would happen if the earl were present and the two men came to blows?

Lucy was occupied with these heavy questions one evening, while Mr. Marlowe, Edward and Lady Philpott played cards. Susanna joined her friend by the sewing table, from which Lucy had drawn a purple thread that rested unused in her hand. Her embroidery in her lap, Lucy gazed absently at Mrs. St. John, who sat apart from the others, refusing to converse or make herself agreeable in any way.

At last, Susanna said to Lucy in exasperation, "I don't see how you brought yourself to rescue this Mrs. St. John. Perhaps you ought to have left her as she was. Why, she is the most disagreeable guest I have ever had the misfortune to entertain. She has not spoken two words to me since her arrival. Is that her idea of gratitude to those who give her a safe haven?"

Sorrowfully, Lucy replied, "I know the lady is difficult to like, but I rescued her, as you put it, because she required rescuing, not because she is likeable. And even if she is disagreeable, she does not deserve to be treated as Mr. Turcott treats her. No one, no matter how ungrateful, deserves such treatment."

Chastened, Susanna replied, "I do not say she deserves ill treatment, only that I should find it difficult to help anyone I disliked so heartily."

"Her education has been faulty, to be sure," Lucy said. "But I do not dislike her. I pity her."

"I do envy your nobility of mind," Susanna declared with a sigh, "for I do not share a particle of it. If a lady were planning to run off with the gentleman I'd set my sights on, I should pull out every hair in her head."

Laughing, Lucy responded, "In the first place, you would do no such thing. When you thought I was going to marry Edward, you were most forbearing. The proof of it is that I still have every hair on my poor head."

At this reference, Susanna took a moment to envy her friend's honey-coloured hair. The maid had swept it up, allowing the curls to frame her oval face. "What is the second place?" she asked.

"It is this: I have not set my sights on Lord Roderick."

"You say you feel towards him as you felt towards Sir Vale."

"I cannot lie to you Susanna. My sentiments towards Lord Roderick are far from indifferent, but I cannot boast of being able to define them any more precisely than that."

As Susanna had never minced a syllable in her life, she said, "I think you are in love with him."

A painful moment followed this assertion, after which Lucy confessed, "Even if I were, it would be unpardonable of me to 'set my sights' on the gentleman. In regard to the female sex, he is many things I cannot admire, and that fact must prevent me from giving in to any inconvenient feelings I might cherish."

"How strong you are, Lucy!"

Lucy knew herself too well to accept such praise. "I'm afraid that where such men as Lord Roderick are concerned, I am guilty of a certain weakness."

For a time, Susanna frowned in thought over what Lucy had said. This matter of the Earl of Silverthorne's character intrigued her, and she wished to know more. To that end, she interrupted Mrs. St.

John's brown study to enquire loudly, "Is it true what one hears, madam? Is Lord Roderick really the scoundrel he is reputed to be?"

The abruptness, not to mention the bluntness, of the question fixed everyone's attention upon the lady who presumably knew the answer.

Lucy placed a restraining hand on Susanna's, but it was too late. The question had been asked and now hung in the air.

Unruffled, Cora St. John returned Susanna's frank look and said, "What may be the conduct of a scoundrel to one lady may have quite a different appearance to another."

"I do not agree," Susanna said with more directness than politeness. "Such a matter does not depend merely on one's opinion, but on the actions of the gentleman in question. A man who is a scoundrel has no principles and does not care whom he hurts to gain his end."

Mrs. St. John replied wearily, "Oh, well, if that is your definition, then we are not speaking of Lord Roderick. A man who has no principles does not befriend a lady in my situation. He does not take it upon himself to effect her escape from an imprudent engagement or to frank her expenses along the way."

Lucy listened to these words with attention, cherishing every syllable she heard to the Earl of Silverthorne's credit.

Mrs. St. John continued, "As to whom he hurts, Lord Roderick is tender not only of his friends—and I include in that number the numerous females of his acquaintance—but he is equally tender of their reputations. I do not exaggerate when I say that my reputation in the world is not all it should be; yet he is

tender of it nonetheless. It may be counted as quix-
otic conduct, but not, I think, the conduct of a
scoundrel.''

Lady Philpott interjected here, ''What Mrs. St.
John says is quite true, Miss Bledsoe. Lord Roderick
is a veritable hero to put himself to so much trouble on
her account.''

Addressing Cora, Lucy said with more emotion
than she intended to betray, ''But he owes you that
much, does he not? After all, he is in part to blame for
your situation with Mr. Turcott. He has compro-
mised you and inflamed the man's temper.''

Cora bit her lip, then replied, ''Because you have
taken me under your protection and because you have
brought me to your friends, I feel obliged to be truthful. Lord Roderick is not the cause of my situation. If
Mr. Turcott did not suspect him, he would suspect
another. He is jealous of all the world, with or without grounds, and I have long since given up hope that
he is to be reasoned with.''

''Then Lord Roderick is blameless?'' Lucy asked.

''In this instance, yes. I, on the other hand, have
behaved abominably. The truth is, from the moment
I learned what Turcott was, I made it a point to behave abominably. You see, my great wish has been
that he would break with me. But he holds me to the
contracts and pursues me relentlessly. I cannot think
why he will not release a lady who makes no secret of
her revulsion for him, but so it is.'' Here her voice
broke.

At this uncharacteristic show of feeling, Lucy went
to Cora St. John, drew up a chair beside her and took
her hand.

As though she had been burned, Cora drew her hand away. "Your good will mortifies me, Miss Bledsoe. Indeed, I was happier when I disliked you and did not have to be grateful."

"I'm sorry," said Lucy.

"Ah, you see, by refusing your kindness, I've behaved abominably again," she said wretchedly. "It appears I can do nothing properly."

Lucy answered warmly, "Your defence of Lord Roderick is very proper, I think. It means a great deal to me."

Cora St. John gave her a bitter smile. In a quiet voice that only Lucy could hear, she said, "Perhaps I shall be able to repay your kindness by taking Roddy out of England. If you were to fall in love with him, you would regret it all of your life."

Putting her hands to her hot cheeks, Lucy watched Mrs. St. John rise and quit the room. The others stared after her in silence.

Gloom hung over the company for a time, causing Mr. Marlowe to yawn and his companions to throw down their cards without finishing the game. Susanna sighed, evidently reflecting that not every woman was as blissfully happy as she was in her marriage to Edward, and Lucy sat near Mrs. St. John's vacant chair, thinking the woman had a very odd notion of repaying a kindness.

Into this bleakness came the servant to announce Lord Roderick, whose name was no sooner uttered than he walked instantly into the saloon, scanning each face until his eyes came to rest on Lucy. His entrance impressed the company with his powerful presence and brought everyone to life. Suddenly the gentlemen wore interested expressions as they rose to greet the newcomer. Lady Philpott, aware that she might get on now with the business of marrying off Lucy, welcomed the earl with a gracious nod. Susanna looked him over from his dark, curled hair to his fine green coat and whispered her approval in Lucy's ear. Lucy nodded a welcome and found herself smiling each time he glanced her way, which he often did.

"We were speaking of you," Susanna informed him when he had taken a chair not far from Lucy's.

"I shall assume that you spoke kindly of me," he said agreeably. "That will prevent your telling me what in fact you did say."

Susanna was not yet prepared to be as agreeable as his lordship. Tartly, she said, "If I recall, there were one or two items mentioned to your credit."

His gaze fell at once on Lucy. "Who is there who can attest anything to my credit?" he asked with a smile.

"Mrs. St. John," Susanna said. Her tone contained a challenge.

At the mention of the name, he stopped smiling. "Ah, Mrs. St. John," he said. "I ought to let her know I have come."

Mr. Marlowe dispatched a servant to inform Mrs. St. John of his lordship's arrival.

"What do you intend to do with the lady?" Susanna enquired.

Lord Roderick took a breath. "I have not yet decided."

Edward said, "I understand that Mr. Turcott may be expected to come looking for Mrs. St. John. I trust you mean to make a decision before he arrives at Edenhurst."

The earl nodded. "I shall come to a decision before the fellow can make himself disagreeable to any of you. You have all been extraordinarily kind, especially Miss Bledsoe."

"You are very quiet, Lucy," Susanna said.

As Lucy's state of high emotion prevented her from disputing this charge, she remained silent. She scolded her heart for fluttering and her tongue for failing. A difficult pause followed and would have persisted for an excruciating time had not Mr. Marlowe pronounced himself ready to retire. Once again, he welcomed Lord Roderick to Edenhurst, then took himself off to bed. It was not long before Lady Philpott retired, too. The newlyweds ought to have followed next, but Susanna informed her husband that she wished to have a word with his lordship.

She had seen as soon as he entered that the earl was as charming as he was handsome, though not so charming and handsome as her Edward. Accordingly, she beckoned Lord Roderick to a window curtained in red and gold, while Edward, who saw that his wife was determined to conduct an interrrogation of the gentleman, talked quietly to Lucy about the weather they had that week, the weather they had that day and the weather they might expect on the morrow.

"I am told," Susanna said, inspecting the gentleman, "that you mean to elope with Mrs. St. John to the Continent."

Though surprised at the declaration, he replied tranquilly, "You have been misinformed."

Pleased with this response, Susanna continued, "I am also given to understand that you have on more

than one occasion behaved like a scoundrel in regard
to the ladies. Am I misinformed on that head, too?''

He laughed. "Not entirely, I'm afraid."

Sternly she said, "That is too bad, sir, too, too
bad.''

"Are you endeavouring to make me reform my
wicked ways?''

She scorned such a suggestion. "I have no intention of reforming your ways, sir. I have all I can do to
reform my own. I have been a hoyden all my life. Now
I am married, however, I mean to behave like a lady.''

Smiling, he said, "Then to what do your questions
tend?''

"I wish to make out your character.''

"But why? I expect to be gone from here in a day,
two at the most. You may never see me again.''

"I do not question you for myself, but on behalf of
my excellent friend Miss Bledsoe. I will not have her
heart broken again. The scoundrel who commits such
an abomination will have to deal with me!''

"Do you think I mean to break her heart?''

"I think you will do so whether you mean to or
not.''

Up to now, the conversation with Susanna Farrineau had proved amusing. The turn it had taken,
however, discomfited him. First his own mother had
begged him to leave Miss Bledsoe alone. Now a
stranger told him without disguise that his interest in
the young woman would likely do her harm.

There were three reasons why these warnings troubled him. First, he had flirted with any number of ladies without doing them any harm; indeed, they
expressed naught but gratitude and delight at his attentions. Second, the last thing he wanted to do was

harm Lucy. He saw plainly that she was far above the generality of women he made love to, and fully proposed to treat her accordingly. And, finally, he sensed more than a germ of truth in the charge and was uncertain himself what he might do, however unintentionally. "What do you wish me to say?" he asked Susanna.

"Promise you will not induce her to fall in love with you."

He half smiled. "Do you believe the promise of a scoundrel is worth anything?"

Susanna liked his directness. "I have no choice but to take your word on the matter."

Gesturing widely, he said gallantly, "As the matter is so important to you and as you have been kind enough to welcome Mrs. St. John in the bosom of your family, I give you my promise. It is the easiest thing in the world, I assure you."

"Thank you. And now I bid you welcome to Edenhurst and good night."

Edward was is the middle of a sentence regarding the prospect of rain when his wife pronounced herself ready to retire. Arm in arm, they walked from the room.

Lucy turned her head to look at Lord Roderick.

He debated coming close to sit near her and decided against it. His recent promise kept him from obeying the impulse that gripped him. Instead, he bade Lucy a cool good-night and made his way to the door.

"Wait," she said. "Please."

He stopped in the open doorway.

"I must know, did you speak with your mother?" she asked.

Keeping his eyes fixed ahead, he replied that he had spoken with her.

"You know everything, then?"

Nodding, he said that he did indeed know everything.

"You are angry with me. I was afraid you would be."

He turned and looked at her. "I am not in the least angry."

"Oh, but you are." she said. "It is perfectly clear. You have scarcely said a word to me since your entrance. Why, you haven't even flirted with me."

He nearly smiled. "I thought you did not like flirting."

"I have never said any such thing. I said I don't know how to flirt. There is a great difference."

In the candlelight, he saw the brightness of her blue eyes. "Thank you for bringing that distinction to my attention. And now, good night."

"Do not go!" she said, stopping him again. She had never seen him behave so distantly or so stiffly towards her and hardly knew what to think.

"I'm afraid I must rest. I have had a long journey."

She stood to say urgently, "There have been men asking after us in the village. They have been seen near Edenhurst. Indeed, they may be lurking about this very minute."

Alert to the possibility that Turcott had found them out, he asked, "You have seen them? Did they threaten you?"

She walked a few steps closer, explaining, "I did not see them myself. Mr. Marlowe's servants saw them.

But I believe Mrs. St. John may have heard them prowling the grounds. She is very much afraid.''

For a moment he considered questioning her further, but recollecting a certain promise, he thought better of it, saying only, ''I shall attend to it in the morning.''

Lucy began to suspect that he was in a hurry to leave her. To test her suspicion, she said, ''It is not very late. I wish you would stay.''

''It is impossible.''

Lucy was certain now that he wished to escape her company and attributed his desire to anger. Despite his earlier denial, she guessed that he had not been able to forgive her for persuading his mother to scheme against him. The thought that she had angered him distressed her deeply. If she could only get him to smile, she thought, they might be on good terms once more. Once that was accomplished, she would be satisfied. She would not even hope to discover what more they might be to one another. So she told herself.

''Lord Roderick,'' she said with an effort, ''I wish to ask you something.''

Expectantly, he turned to her once more.

In desperation, Lucy tried to think of a question to ask him. Nothing came to her.

''You may ask me anything you like,'' he said gently.

She took a breath. ''This is very difficult.''

Touched by her difficulty, he removed his hand from the door to say, ''You may trust me.''

She coloured, ransacked her mind and found it devoid of everything except the certainty that she could not allow him to leave her.

''What did you wish to speak of?'' he prompted.

Opening her full lips, she heard herself say, "Flirting."

He could not help but smile. "You have chosen your subject well. It is one in which I am known to be thoroughly versed. What did you wish to say in regard to flirting?"

She would have been at a loss to answer had she not hit on the idea of saying, "I thought perhaps you would be willing to take a moment to teach me how to flirt. If I knew the proper method of performing it, I daresay I should not find the practise so alarming."

He laughed.

She looked down. "I see. You think I could not learn it. You think I would make a perfectly ridiculous flirt."

Unable to stop himself, he came to her. "I don't think that at all."

Meeting his eyes, she said, "Very well then, will you teach me?"

"I wouldn't know where to begin. It requires a certain artfulness to be a creditible flirt."

"I assure you, I am as artful as anyone. You have seen me act the part of your Canterbury miss. Was that not artfulness?"

"That was different. Your object was to teach me a lesson."

"And did you learn a lesson?"

"More than one."

She detected another smile in his tone. "Excellent," she said, "then you owe me a lesson in return, and the one I wish to learn is flirting. Pray, what am I to do first?"

He was irresistibly entertained by the idea of instructing Miss Bledsoe in the art of flirting. Therefore, he replied, "I suppose we might discuss the philosophy of it. One should understand the fundamental concept of any discipline. Then the practical application follows logically."

Lucy folded her hands and listened with an air of rapt attention.

Charmed by her student's pose, he instructed, "The first object of flirting is to win notice, to make the gentlemen aware of you. They must know when you have entered a room or left it. While you remain, their eyes must be on you."

"How do I accomplish that?"

"In any number of ways: by dress, manner, conversation."

She looked down at her dress with a frown. Gesturing helplessly, she said, "I suppose this dress will not do."

For a considerable time, he appraised the dress, which was a pale blue muslin, cut round below the neck and ornamented with delicate puffed sleeves and a lavender ribbon under the bosom. He noted, not for the first time, how Miss Bledsoe's gown clung to her slender figure. "Your dress will do very well," he said, congratulating himself upon his restraint.

"My manner, then. What should I do to improve my manner?" Here she looked at him with an expression which stopped him. He had never known a woman who blended earnestness with humour as bewitchingly as Lucy Bledsoe. "Your manner requires no improvement," he assured her. "I should not like to see you alter it in any way."

This reply pleased Lucy enough to prompt her to draw closer to him. "Then we must do something about my conversation. I am hopeless there, as you well know. Telling a gentleman he is a scoundrel is not at all the thing. I am sure you would advise against it.''

''Not in the least. Such an assertion is sure to succeed in getting his attention.''

''Which is the object of flirting, is it not?'' she pointed out brightly.

''There,'' he said. ''You have learned the first lesson to perfection.''

Although she had already won several smiles from him, she was far from ready to put a period to their conversation. ''What is the second lesson?'' she asked.

By this time, she had drawn so close that he had to put his hands behind his back to keep from touching her. ''The second lesson is never to be serious about any of the gentlemen who attend to you. Insincerity is the very hallmark of the flirt.''

Wrinkling her forehead, she studied the idea for a time. ''I see. You mean that I am to act one way and feel another?''

''Precisely.''

''As you did when you kissed me in the hall at Lever Combe?''

''*What?*'' he thundered.

His amazement was delicious. Quietly she said, ''Mrs. St. John assured me that your kiss was wholly insincere, intended merely to persuade the onlookers that I was engaged to you.''

''You ought to have asked *my* opinion, not Mrs. St. John's,'' he said between his teeth.

''I should be very interested to hear your opinion,'' she replied. Then she smiled at him.

As if they had a will of their own, his arms went tightly around her and pressed her close. His mouth found hers. His hands held her as though she might be taken from him if he did not hold on for dear life. Concerned that he might have hurt her by the intensity of his embrace, he let go. Then, finding her wearing an expression of delight, he let his fingers wander to her neck and cheeks. He would have pulled her to him again, except that his mother's warnings and his recent promise to Susanna inconveniently crowded into his head. At once, he released her.

She drew away, and while he took a moment to renew his resolve, she felt all the luxury of being desired. With gentle archness, she said, "I cannot have learned my lesson very well. You evidently do not wish to continue. Perhaps you can point out my errors. I shall do my best to correct them."

"Lucy," he said firmly, "it is time for you to go to bed."

Seeing the uncharacteristic gravity on his face, she asked, "What is wrong?"

"I have never resisted a woman in my life," he said. "Don't make this more difficult for me than it already is."

She would have put a soothing hand on his arm, but they were interrupted by Mrs. St. John, who marched into the room saying, "Well, Roddy, you've come at last!"

CHAPTER ELEVEN

Danger

THEY LOOKED ROUND to see Mrs. St. John standing in the open doorway. She greeted the earl with the first sign of animation she had shown in some time. Lucy was forced to step away from his side as Cora St. John demanded his attention.

Lord Roderick, determined to send Lucy from the room as quickly as possible, greeted Mrs. St. John with an excess of civility. He raised one of her hands to his lips, then the other, behaving as if he had forgotten Lucy's presence. He appeared wholly absorbed in questioning the beautiful widow about her health, her state of mind and her manner of entertaining herself in his absence. Not waiting for the answer to one question, he fired off another.

Lucy saw that she had no choice but to leave them together. Reluctantly, she said good-night; neither of them seemed to hear her. When she walked slowly through the open door, turning her head to see if Lord Roderick noticed her exit, she saw that he was occupied in inducing Mrs. St. John to sit with him on the sofa. That sight caused her to reflect that if the object of flirtation was to be noticed when one entered and left a room, then she was no match for Mrs. St. John.

Mortified, she went at once up the grand staircase to her chamber.

Dismissing the chambermaid, Lucy seated herself at the dressing table. For a time, she contemplated her woeful image in the glass. She saw tears streak her cheeks and brushed them away. Dissatisfied with the pining creature who stared back at her, she made a moue. "Lady Philpott will give you a scold if you cry your eyes red," she warned the young lady who faced her.

Much as she tried not to, she could not help recollecting Lord Roderick's words. They came back to her with a sharper sting than she had felt at the moment he uttered them. He had never resisted a woman before, he had told her. She was the only woman he had ever in his life refused! The whole world knew that he made love to women short and tall, buxom and thin, young and old, married and unmarried, charming and dull, pretty and plain—but he declined to make love to her. It was humiliating.

She might have shed more tears over this mortifying thought had it not occurred to her to ask why Lord Roderick should suddenly decide to do what he had never done before in his life. Why should a man who believed that the sole purpose of temptation was to submit to it now declare his intention to resist? Why should he kiss her the way a hungry child eats apple tarts, and then refrain from kissing her again? Why should a man with a reputation for being a scoundrel with the ladies suddenly behave like a perfect gentleman?

Only one answer came to her. It seemed as inescapable as it was unbelievable, and it caused her to glance again at the face in the glass, this time with a smile.

LORD RODERICK, meanwhile, attended assiduously to Mrs. St. John until Lucy had gone. The moment she disappeared, he stood, paced and said with determination, "I suppose it would be best if I did take you to the Continent."

She gazed at him cynically. "I will not go to the Continent with you, Roddy. I will not go anywhere with you."

"I thought you wished to elope. Do you mean to say you intend to jilt me now that I've come round to your way of thinking?"

"You have no wish to elope with me. You are in love with Lucy Bledsoe."

Irritably he replied, "I wish you would not bring up love, Cora. You know it gives me dyspepsia."

"I stood in that doorway a long time, and you did not notice I was there."

"Regardless of whether I love the lady or not, I've promised to stay as far from her as possible. My proximity, it seems, will only break her fragile heart."

"Ha! Miss Bledsoe's heart is as fragile as Gibraltar, and I do not think she wishes you to keep as far from her as possible."

"That is the irony in our situation. I have to look out for her best interests, since she will not do it herself. A fitting punishment for a scoundrel, I daresay: to be forced to protect the very lady he has set his sights on."

"That is precisely why I will not go away with you. You look out for my *reputation*, which is already a hopeless shambles, but you look out for Miss Bledsoe's *heart*."

He regarded her. Then, in a kinder voice, he asked, "What will you do, Cora? You are not thinking of returning to London?"

"No. I cannot return. Turcott will never leave me in peace. I must go away and hope that he will soon give over any further idea of plaguing me."

"You must leave Edenhurst at once, I'm sorry to say. Turcott appears to be on our trail, and we have no time to lose in getting you to safety. By morning I shall have thought of a plan to get you to the north."

"Perhaps I shall like being alone better than I had thought."

He paused a moment before saying, "I suppose I shall have to speak with Miss Bledsoe. She will have to know of our intention to get you away from Edenhurst."

"Did you not tell me a minute ago that you meant to avoid her?"

"I owe her the courtesy of telling her. She has, after all, gone to considerable bother for our sakes."

She eyed him knowingly. "That is very commendable, Roddy, to be sure."

"You will have to act as chaperon, my dear."

She was dismayed. "Are you daft? I, a chaperon?"

"Yes. She will not protect herself and, as an incorrigible scoundrel, I cannot be trusted to do it." To Mrs. St. John's horror, he smiled, kissed her hand and announced blithely, "There is nothing for it, Cora, but that you be the one to protect your protector."

AT DAWN, Lucy burrowed into her featherdown pillows with a luxurious sense of pleasure, but before she could recollect the source of it, she heard a scratching at her door. She could not imagine who would knock at such an hour. Slowly the door opened and Susanna came in. Still wearing her nightclothes and cap, she climbed upon the soft bed next to Lucy, saying quietly, as though someone in the room still slept, "I am glad you are awake, for I must have your advice, Lucy."

Lucy sat up against her pillows and promised to do her best to invent some advice worth heeding. "In most cases there is not much danger of one's advice being heeded, and so the temptation is to say exactly what one thinks, but one can never count on being ignored." She had expected Susanna to laugh with her at this sally, but her friend frowned.

"I wish you would be serious," Susanna said. "I am in a pickle, and I have put off saying anything for too long."

Lucy wished with all her heart to be serious, but last night's astounding discovery made it impossible. "I will try," she promised but had to put up her hand to hide a smile.

"As you know," Susanna said, "I have not been Mrs. Farrineau for very many weeks. When Edward and I were married, we did not wish to take our honeymoon immediately. The first wish of our hearts was to care for my father, whose years in the West Indies had given him a touch of fever, and to see him reestablished in comfort at Edenhurst."

Lucy knew how attached Susanna was to her father. She said warmly, "How much pleasure it must give you to see that your care and companionship have restored him to good health."

"Oh, yes, but we never forgot that we were still to have a honeymoon. You did not know this—for I forbade anyone to mention it—but the day you arrived was the day before Edward, Father and I were to set forth on that very honeymoon.''

"I am so sorry,'' Lucy said, regretting with all her heart that she had put her friends to so much inconvience.

"It was clear that you and Mrs. St. John were in some difficulty. We could not run off and leave you.''

"It is one thing for *me* to make sacrifices for Mrs. St. John—that is my choice—but there was no reason for you to make any. Susanna, I am very sorry.'' Lucy made up her mind on the spot to take Mrs. St. John from Edenhurst that very day, though she had no idea where she would take her to.

"Well, it *was* a great sacrifice; I admit it without disguise,'' Susanna allowed. "However, I could not leave Edenhurst before I'd had a look at this Lord Roderick of yours.''

Deeply curious, Lucy asked, "Susanna, now you have had your look, what is your opinion? Do you like him?''

"Of course he is nothing to Edward, though he is taller and somewhat broader in the shoulders, but he might be made into something, for he is awfully dashing. If anyone could do it, Lucy, it would be you.''

"It sounds to me,'' Lucy said gently, "as though you have come here to give advice, not to ask it.''

"I haven't got to the advice part yet. You must be patient and let me continue.''

Once again Lucy endeavoured not to smile.

Susanna went on: "As our trunks have been in readiness for a week now, and as there is another ship sailing in two days, we have decided it is now time for us to depart on our honeymoon, and we should like to invite Mrs. St. John to accompany us."

Amazed, Lucy cried, "You wish to take Mrs. St. John to the Continent?"

"Not to the Continent; to the West Indies. Father has promised to show us his sugar-cane plantation."

"But you do not like Mrs. St. John."

"That is true, but I have taken a page from your book and tried to learn a bit of compassion, and I do see that the woman is dreadfully frightened, as well she should be, and fear is not likely to make one very cordial, is it? Once she is at sea and safe from discovery, I expect we shall find her more agreeable. And she will be able to repay my extraordinary kindness to her by playing cards with my father and amusing him while Edward and I are occupied."

Lucy drew in her breath. "It certainly answers my difficulty and Lord Roderick's wonderfully well."

"What I wish to know is whether you adivse me to pursue the scheme."

"There is nothing I should like better than to see your scheme succeed, but I'm afraid Mrs. St. John will never agree. Her heart is set on an elopement with Lord Roderick."

This objection weighed not at all with Susanna, now that she had won Lucy's approval. She climbed off the bed, walked with a bouncing step to the door and before she closed it behind her, declared roundly, "Then we shall simply have to change her mind, won't we!"

She was still smiling at Susanna's parting remark when Lucy heard another scratching at her chamber door. This time the visitor proved to be Lady Philpott, who, far from wearing nightclothes, was sumptuously attired in a purple morning dress. "A word with you, my dear girl," said her ladyship, settling herself in a sturdy chair.

Lucy removed her nightcap and let her curls fall free, preparing to hear her out.

"Of late, dear girl, we have not had as many opportunities for conversation as I could wish. Therefore, I've not been able to whisper a caution in your ear."

"I hope I am cautious, even without such generous reminders."

"With regard to most matters, I am sure you are as cautious as a sensible girl should be. But on one subject, I very much fear you may have been prejudiced by the past." Here Lady Philpott fixed her with an expression full of pathos.

Intrigued, Lucy waited to hear more.

"I do not wish to pain you by alluding to the tragic events which recently took place in Bath. Still, I am obliged to say that as a result of them, you have tended to regard the male species with rather more suspicion than would otherwise be in your nature. I fear that in so doing you may fail to recognize a gentleman who may cherish a sincere regard for you."

"Oh, my. I had forgotten Bath, until you mentioned it." Lucy's earlier happiness threatened to cloud; however, she refused to let memories oppress her. She had the future entirely in view, a future in which Lord Roderick figured vaguely but importantly.

"I speak most particularly of remarks I have heard Mrs. St. John make with regard to Lord Roderick and his conduct towards you. I believe the lady observed on one occasion that his kissing you at Lever Combe was a sham. Well, I hope you did not believe her. Her opinion is not to be trusted any more than her character.''

With a gently teasing smile, Lucy said, ''She also observed that his lordship was very brave in befriending her and remaining loyal. Am I to disbelieve her there, too?''

Lady Philpott, who did not regard the subject at hand as a joking matter, replied, ''Oh, no! That you may believe. It is the other business—the business about the kiss—that you are not to believe.''

''Dear Lady Philpott,'' Lucy said affectionately, ''put your mind at rest. I can assure you I do not fret about the kisses Lord Roderick gives. It is the kisses he refuses to give that interest me!''

Lady Philpott's jaw dropped. Her heart sank. She had been certain that Lucy was in love with Lord Roderick. On that conviction, she had agreed to swoof off to Worcestershire. Now she heard that the girl was not the least interested in the gentleman or his kisses. Never in her life had she so misjudged.

It seemed impossible that a young woman who had fallen in love with Sr. Vale Saunders could resist the charms of a man so superior in every way. It seemed impossible that Lucy's broken heart was beyond mending. It seemed impossible that she, Lady Philpott, was destined to change her mind once more. But so it was.

Feeling aged, weary and aching in her bones, her ladyship rose from the chair to take herself from the room. She had wished to catch an earl for her young companion. Instead she had caught the gentleman for Cora St. John, whose intended husband might appear at any moment to shoot their heads off and sub-

ject them to heaven knew what other indignities. Lady
Philpott could not recall when she had felt so low.

THE GENTLEMEN OFFERED several objections to Susanna's proposal. Edward thought Mrs. St. John's
escaping to the West Indies would purchase freedom
at too great a price. The lady ought to stay in England, where the contracts she had signed could be
contested on her behalf. He had no doubt that fraud
could be proved against Turcott and her fortune re-
gained. But if she left England, she might as well give
it up.

Mr. Marlowe very much feared that in the islands
Mrs. St. John would fall victim to fever, as he had
done.

Lord Roderick did not know whether Mrs. St. John
would like travelling with strangers, imposing on their
good will and living in a dependent condition for a
considerable time.

The first voice in favour of the scheme was Lady
Philpott's. It occurred to her that Lucy might possibly be persuaded to interest herself in Lord Roderick's kisses were Mrs. St. John removed to the other
side of the ocean. Her hopes of making Lucy a countess instantly revived. Loudly she declared Susanna's
plan remarkably sensible. She stated that she would be
happy to put her own solicitor to work in an effort to
nullify the marriage contracts with Turcott. If there
was any justice at all in this vale of tears, Mrs. St. John
would be allowed to have her own money back again.
In the meantime, a sojourn in the West Indies would
rather improve her health and colour so that she might
catch herself another husband soon.

Her ladyship was pleased to hear Lucy add her persuasions to the debate. Gently, she suggested that Mrs.
St. John might welcome the opportunity to go among
strangers who did not know her circumstances and
would not judge her harshly.

The argument went back and forth for a time until
Mrs. St. John rose from her chair to say that she had
a fancy to see the West Indies; there was nothing she
would like better than to put her foolish life behind her
and begin a new one in the New World.

"The matter is settled, then," said her ladyship,
smacking her lips and promising herself that she would
see Lucy the earl's bride or give up matchmaking for
the rest of eternity.

Arrangements were promptly made for a quick departure on the morrow. As Cora St. John followed the
others from the room, Lord Roderick whispered to
her, "Stay a moment. I must speak with Miss Bledsoe."

"I must go and pack my things," she whispered
back.

"Cora, may I remind you that you promised to act
as chaperon."

Betraying not a shred of remorse, she said, "I have
already been guilty of one breach of promise to a
gentleman. I daresay another will not be remarked."
On that, she went out in search of the maid and her
trunk.

Although he wished to avoid a tête-à-tête with Lucy,
one which would subject him to the temptations inspired by her lovely presence, Lord Roderick felt
compelled to discuss with her their own arrangements. Therefore, he stood by the japanned screen and

observed her at the table, sewing a piece of work. "Where will you go now?" he asked.

She replied, "I believe Lady Philpott will wish to return to Queenscroft. And you?"

As he had determined to go wherever Lucy did not, he said, "Business may take me to Town." Then he moved to the window where he looked out upon a pleasant prospect of sloping ground dewy with rain.

Lucy saw his uneasiness. It left her breathless to think that the man noted for his insouciance with the ladies could betray real discomfort in her presence. "I had hoped you, too, would wish to visit your mother," she said softly.

"I have just come from her. She will give me a scold if I turn up again so soon."

She put her work aside and went to the window, standing just behind him. "I should be grateful for your escort, now that Lord Knatchbull's servants have returned to Lever Combe. If Turcott should attack us, I do not know how Lady Philpott and I and our poor frightened maids should defend ourselves."

He turned to give her a grave look before moving past her, and as her request was perfectly logical, he said, "Very well, my servants and I shall accompany you to Canterbury." On this, he went to the door.

"Lord Roderick," she said, and though she spoke gently, she succeeded in stopping him, "I do believe you wish to avoid my company."

He wondered that he could find a lady who was so sincere, so goodhearted, so impulsively open—in short, so unlike himself—so damnably attractive. In the bantering tone he had often used at Lever Combe, he replied, "My dearest bride, if I avoid your charming company, it is only because I wish to practice being

married. The very hallmark of a polite husband is to
inflict his presence on his wife as little as possible. If
it were not, I assure you, there would be no getting rid
of me."

As Lucy watched him perform an exaggerated bow
and stride from the room, she smiled at his eloquent
lie.

THE NEXT MORNING witnessed an affectionate, tear-
ful leavetaking. Before climbing into the carriage,
Cora St. John squeezed Lucy's hand and said, "I have
done nothing but protest your kindness. Today, I
thank you for it." When Lucy would not be thanked,
Cora added, "For your sake, I wish I could have kept
my promise to whisk Roderick out of England. You
are in grave danger, I fear, for he is in love with you."
On that, the carriage departed for the port of Sou-
thampton, leaving Lucy to exult in the knowledge that
she was loved.

MOMENTS LATER, the second carriage departed for the
county of Kent. Lord Roderick declined to join the
ladies. Instead, he rode his stalwart chestnut and kept
well in front of the carriage so as to put it out of his
power to catch a glimpse of Lucy's face through the
window. Although she was particularly fetching that
day in a green peaked bonnet, he was determined to
give temptation a good battle. Therefore, in the afternoon, after they had stopped to rest the horses and
partake of refreshment, he announced his intention to
ride ahead to ensure the safety of their route.

Half an hour after she had lost sight of Lord Roderick along the road, Lucy heard riders approaching.

The sound came from behind the carriage and was accompanied by whoops and shouts that alarmed her.

"Good heavens, banditti!" cried Lady Philpott. Instinctively, she patted her bosom, where she customarily hid a stocking full of jewels whenever she travelled. To her relief, the stocking was in place.

The carriage was brought to an abrupt halt. Peering outside the window, Lucy saw a horde of masked highwaymen, caped in black, holding pistols pointed at her and the coachman.

"I suppose they want us to stand and deliver," whispered Lady Philpott. "We had better do as they say." Knowing that her jewels were safely hidden, she was well disposed to comply with any request to hand over her reticule, in which she carried only a few shillings.

When Lucy implored the gentlemen to do no harm to her ladyship and the two trembling maids, one of the ruffians pulled her roughly from the carriage. Daintily she composed her person and repeated her plea to the four men who sat on frisky horses and glared at the ladies from behind masks. As soon as the women stood outside the carriage, the leader of the banditti gave a nod of his head. Two fellows climbed down from their mounts and approached the ladies, coming so close to Lady Philpott that she clasped one hand to her bosom. With the other, she held out her reticule.

One of the men stared at the reticule. "What the deuce is this?" he snarled.

"She's giving you her pin money, fool," said the other man. "Well, take it!"

"What the devil do I want with a lady's purse?" He flung it back at her ladyship, who now grew alarmed, to think that they were after bigger profit. Rather than suffer the loss of her jewels, not to mention the dignity of her person, Lady Philpott stepped to the leader, looked up at him defiantly, and said, "I have been singularly patient with you gentlemen, even going so far as to save you the trouble of demanding my money. I expect a certain civility in return."

"Quiet!" the leader demanded. Dismounting, he went to the carriage to inspect its empty compartment. When he had done, he announced, "She is not here."

Immediately, Lucy recognized the surly voice of Mr. Turcott. She turned to him, nearly out of breath with indigation, saying, "It is true. Mrs. St. John is not here. She is not where you will ever find her."

He came so close to Lucy that she received a strong and disagreeable impression of drink.

"I shall have her arrested," he threatened. "I shall say she has stolen items of great value from me. They will bring her back and jail her."

"Good heavens! Is that Mr. Turcott?" Lady Philpott cried.

Pulling off his mask, the man favoured her with a scowl. "What have you done with Cora St. John?"

"I am so relieved to see you," cried Lady Philpott. "I am sure you do not wish to steal my poor jewels."

Exasperated, the fellow shouted, "I don't give a groat for your jewels. But if you do not held your tongue, I shall strangle you."

This pronouncement caused something of a stir among the other gentlemen. After a brief consultation, one of them walked to Turcott to say, "If we can't get the lady, we may as well take the damned jewels."

"I wish you would mind your language," Lady Philpott reprimanded him. "Remember there are ladies present."

The fellow would have given her ladyship the back of his hand, but Lucy drew her away.

"The devil with jewels," Turcott cried. "We are after a sly fox." On that, he seized Lucy by the arms and demanded, "Tell me where she is, or I will shake it out of you."

After glancing at his hand on her arm, she said with a sigh, "I suppose there is no hope of persuading you to listen to reason. I have witnessed enough of your behaviour towards Mrs. St. John to know that you cannot be induced to be merciful. All I ask is that you consider whether you wish to be brought up on charges—by myself and Lady Philpott."

It took a moment for the meaning of this threat to penetrate Turcott's skull, for it was delivered in the gentlest tone. When the threat did at last sink in, he tried another tactic. Releasing her, he said, "I expect she's gone with Roderick. To find her, I need only look for him."

This announcement startled Lucy, who knew that Lord Roderick had ridden ahead alone and that if the highwaymen should come upon him, he would be in the gravest danger. "She is not with him," Lucy said.

"Then where the devil is she?"

Seeing no other way out, Lucy replied, "She has sailed to the West Indies."

He laughed uproariously. "You make a poor liar, Miss Bledsoe. Now I am certain she has gone with him."

For an instant, she despaired. Then it occurred to her to say, with a bowed head and a voice she hoped was pathetic, "You have found me out, sir. I was lying. Lord Roderick has taken Mrs. St. John to the village of Cheedham."

Another laugh followed this declaration. "We have just come from Cheedham. We saw no one there resembling a fashionable gentleman and his mistress." On that, he swung himself upon his horse, calling to his men, "Well, laddies, she wishes to send us to Cheedham. She wants us to go back. Therefore, we must go forward." Laughing again, he signalled to his followers and galloped down the road.

When the sound of hoofbeats had faded, Lucy implored the coachman to follow them.

Appalled, the man replied, "We have got off easy this time, miss. No telling what they may do to us if they clap eyes on us again."

"But they've gone after Lord Roderick. They may hurt him."

He agreed that such an event would be sad indeed. "But," he added, "better that only one should be hurt than all of us."

"While we are debating," Lucy cried, "those villains may be in the act of attacking Lord Roderick. They would not scruple to kill him if he resists, and he is certain to resist."

Although the coachman believed devoutly in the doctrine of saving one's own skin, he was not so hardhearted as to wish the death of Lord Roderick, who had generously given him a few coins when they had set out from Edenhurst. He therefore bade the footman assist the ladies into the carriage once more, and off they sped along the road, where the dust that had been kicked up by the highwaymen's horses still hung in the air.

The pace could not be as fast as Lucy wished, owing to a sudden narrowing of the path. They passed through a copse of trees and shrubs, which rendered the road momentarily dark. Around a bend, they attained open country again. Considerably ahead, they saw something in the road: a bundle of rags, it appeared to be at first, then a gentleman's cape, then a gentleman wearing a cape. Slowing, the carriage drew near the still figure; the coachman reined the horses to a stop. Without waiting for the footman to open the door, Lucy jumped from the carriage and ran to Lord Roderick.

He lay on his side, eyes closed, his fine profile catching the sunlight. His forehead had sustained an ugly gash. One arm was bleeding heavily. She could not tell where else he had been wounded, and she did not wish to move him lest she do further harm. Brushing tears from her cheeks, she begged the ladies to give her their handkerchiefs, which they did not hesitate to do; likewise, the servants offered theirs.

Lucy tied several of the linens together to make a tourniquet. Gently, she reached it under and around the earl's wounded arm. As she did so, her cheek brushed against his hair, and she paused to look into his impassive face. The movement of his chest assured her that he still breathed, but the stillness of his face frightened her.

Tying the remaining handkerchiefs together, she tenderly bound his forehead. When the knot was fixed, she touched his cheeks soothingly. To her joy, he opened his eyes and looked at her. He was oblivious to the others who stared down at him. All he knew was that he wished to reach for the green ribbon adorning Lucy's bonnet and could not move his arm.

"What have I been drinking?" he asked. "I feel as if I'd been shot in the head."

"I expect you have been shot in the head, my lord," Lucy said softly.

"You did not shoot me, I hope?"

Patiently she assured him that she had not shot him.

"Then I suppose your husband shot me."

As calmly as she could, she said, "I have no husband."

With difficulty, he said, "Do you know, you have the most astonishing blue eyes."

She smiled. "Are you flirting with me, sir?"

"Ah, it is you, Lucy." He closed his eyes.

"Yes."

"Stay here beside me. It is imperative that we talk."

"You are lying on the highway, my lord. We shall be run over by the next carriage that comes along."

"In that case, we shall defer our discussion for a more agreeable setting." He coughed painfully.

Signalling the coachmen and servants, Lucy whispered a few instructions. Then, turning to the earl once more, she said in a quiet voice, "You are going to be moved now. Every effort will be made to move you gently, but I'm afraid we cannot entirely spare you pain."

The footman and coachman assisted him to his feet. Lucy entered the carriage so that she might make him easy when he was lifted inside. The exertions of the move were so great as to cause him to slump against her in a faint. When, sometime later, he recovered consciousness, he was aware of the rocking motion of the coach and of a fragrant softness supporting his head. Blissfully, he slept a few minutes. Waking, he again became aware of the warmth that pillowed him.

"Don't try to move," he heard Lucy's voice say, and as she spoke, he could feel the vibrations of her words against his cheek. It struck him now that he rested his cheek on the exquisite bosom of Miss Lucy Bledsoe, whom he had promised his mother, Susanna Farrineau, and, most of all, himself, to keep at a safe distance. Smiling, he nestled closer to her and consigned those promises to hell.

CHAPTER TWELVE

The Chambermaid

AT LUCY'S DIRECTION, the coachman raced the horses until an inn hove into view. The carriage pulled up in the yard of the Blandish Arms Inn, Hostelry and Public House, where the innkeeper and a number of chickens came running and squawking to greet the new arrivals. Lucy lost no time in having his lordship carried to a room and a surgeon sent for. When he arrived, Lady Philpott insisted upon cross-examining him on the earl's state of health.

Piously, the balding surgeon folded his hands across his large middle, grimaced at Lord Roderick, who lay sleeping in the best bed the inn could provide, and intoned, "His lordship has sustained a head wound inflicted by a bullet, which, happily, only grazed the epidermis. I removed a second bullet from his upper right limb. In addition, he has suffered a severe bruise on the right hip, precipitated by a fall. It is my conclusion that the Earl of Silverthorne is unlikely to live out the night."

This pronouncement caused Lucy to utter a cry.

"Stuff!" said Lady Philpott in disgust. "You fellows like to sentence every man to death. Then, when he miraculously recovers, you ask for twice the money, claiming it was your skill that saved the wretched creature."

Offended, the surgeon denied the charge, while Lucy gazed at Lord Roderick's pale countenance and tried to imagine that powerful energy snuffed out.

"You will get no money out of us beyond what is due," her ladyship warned the surgeon. "I will not be gouged by quackery."

On hearing this vow, the surgeon revised his diagnosis. Lord Roderick, he said, might suffer a fever and some dizziness owing to the injury to his head. In all other respects, he appeared healthy enough to be up and about before many days.

It was well that the surgeon did revise his diagnosis, for an hour after it was delivered, his lordship awoke and found that he was hungry. Ringing the bell, he summoned the publican, who soon brought him a dinner of beefsteak, roast fowl, joint of ham and oysters. He addressed his meal with relish, only to find that he could not move his right arm and could not cut his meat with his left. He was on the point of eating with his hands, when Lucy slipped into the room.

Although it was a small chamber, it was neat and cozy. Over the bed, the ceiling peaked in a triangle supported by a dark wooden beam of monstrous size. From the beam hung a lamp that painted the walls with flickering shadows. Noticing the closeness in the room, Lucy tiptoed to the other side of the bed to open the casement. She turned from the window to see that he was awake. "How do you do?" she asked.

Smiling, he replied, "I am reduced to eating in the manner of a barbarian, ripping my meat to pieces with my teeth. Should word of such doings get out, I shall be banned from Boodles."

"I shall cut your meat," she said. Demurely she brought a chair to the bedside and sat. Inspecting the contents of the tray on his lordship's lap, she leaned forward to cut his meat. She took a forkful of beef and raised it to his lips, which parted expectantly. Their eyes met. Seeing his smile, she paused with the fork in midair. He shut his mouth and his smile grew broader. His eyes held hers. The next time he opened his mouth, the fork moved to its intended destination.

In silence, she continued with the feeding, which was frequently interrupted with looks and smiles. When he had eaten his fill, Lord Roderick watched her remove the tray and carry it to a table. Then he said, "I suppose you had better tell me what information you gave Turcott."

"I told him the truth, but he did not believe me."

Satisfaction lit his face. "It is no more than he deserves. Happily I got off one or two excellent hits to his abdomen and nose before he started waving his pistol in the air."

"He might have killed you."

He laughed. "It is fortunate he did not kill me, for if he had, who would teach you to flirt?"

Coming close to the bed, she responded, "It appears I am never to learn the art, for you have avoided my company ever since I proposed that you teach me."

He saw her standing in the half light, her face barely visible. "You proved a quick study. I soon saw that you are fully ready to flirt with the best of them."

Taking a step, she came into the light. "Such praise from the master is flattering indeed, but you mistake me. I was not flirting. I was entirely in earnest."

"In that case," he said quietly, "give me your hand."

When she complied, he pulled her down to him so that he might kiss her. Once or twice he moaned, when one of his wounds was touched; but on the whole, he considered it the most exquisite of pleasures to caress Lucy with his good arm.

It was not long before their kisses grew fervid, so that Lucy's delight in them began to stir other sensations. She could feel his ardour increasing. At the same time, she could hear murmurs of "ouch" at numerous inappropriate moments. With each stab of pain, she kissed him again, until, all at once, she felt a stab of pain within herself, a pain as physical as any Lord Roderick experienced, a pain which blocked her throat and told her that she was doing precisely what she had vowed not to do: she was falling in love with a scoundrel.

Indeed, she could no longer deceive herself; she had been in love with him almost from the first.

A voice told her that he was not a scoundrel, not entirely at any rate; that he had behaved honorably in many instances, though the press of his lips on hers momentarily chased those instances from her mind; and that he did sincerely love her, as witnessed by his late attempt to resist her.

But another voice told her that his resistance had been suspiciously short-lived; that he might behave honorably in all sorts of instances but had given no indication of having reformed his ways with women; that, in fact, his kisses and caresses, which fired her more every second, only indicated that his ways with women had now successfully extended to her.

The first voice scolded her for letting suspicion get in the way of sensation; the second, for rushing headlong into another affair of the heart which would give

Canterbury further reason to gossip and regard her with compassionate stares. The first voice whispered that she ought to lose herself in the moment, a moment she had been denied too long, a moment she had wished for with all her heart. The other whispered that she was an arrant fool.

Pulling away, Lucy put her hands to her ears so as to fend off the voices. She stood, breathing hard, endeavouring to quell her emotion. When he reached for her, his eyes hot, she drew back. Smiling sadly, she said, "I must say good-night."

"Apparently my inclinations overcame my judgement just now," he remarked in a velvet voice.

"I forgive you," she answered quickly. She had the sense that the room had grown stifling in the last minute.

"It was your own fault, you know," he said.

"No doubt it was," she said, catching her breath.

"If you had not responded as you did, I should not have gone so far."

Eagerly, she reassured him, "I do not blame you; please believe that. I only wish you a restful sleep and a speedy recovery." She went to the door.

He threw off the blanket deliberately. As she watched him get out of the bed and walk to her, she felt the effort each movement cost him.

"You cannot leave a dying man," he said when he reached her. The playfulness in his eyes was irresistible.

Mustering a calm voice, she said, "Lady Philpott has forced the surgeon to declare that you will live."

"But you cannot leave a man who loves you as I do."

Astonished, she gazed at him. She had guessed that he loved her; she had heard Cora St. John confirm the fact. But she had never dreamed he would go so far as to say so. Profoundly moved, she said, "I am not insensible of the honour you do me by saying what you have just said. A man who must invent a Canterbury tale in order to ward off entanglements with the ladies does not utter such words lightly."

"I am glad you appreciate the rarity of my words. You intend to reward them, I trust." He brought her hand to his lips, kissing her palm.

Helplessly, she said, "I love you, too, Roderick. And now, goodbye."

His lordship was not accustomed to young ladies running off just when events promised to prove interesting. Therefore, he objected, "You cannot simply disappear, Lucy. I haven't got accustomed to hearing myself say that I love you. You must allow me to repeat it four or five thousand times."

She shook her head. "I dare not allow you one more minute. It will not do for me to love you and for you to love me. It is a condition full of danger. I am weary of danger. I am weary of having it whispered that I have been crossed in love. I do not wish to be pitied ever again. I shall ask Lady Philpott to find me an elderly, fat widower who adores and worships only me, and I shall marry him as soon as the settlements can be drawn up."

Laughing, he said, "I forbid you to marry such a lout."

If she had not wished to weep, she would have smiled. "Let me go, Roderick, I beg you. If you do not, I shall be lost."

"I cannot let you marry that gluttonous old widower, my love. I mean to marry you myself."

There was a silence during which she wondered if she had heard aright.

"I hope you have noticed," he remarked, "that I have just proposed marriage. It would be a great pity if such a grand declaration were to be entirely thrown away."

Touching his cheek, she said, "You may withdraw the proposal, Roderick. It will be as though I had never heard it, if you wish."

Warmly, he slipped his hand round her waist and pressed her close. "You did hear it," he said. "If you stay a moment, you shall hear it again."

By way of reply, she threw her arms about his neck, kissing him wildly on the ears and mouth, luxuriating in the silky touch of his lips on her neck and shoulders. Now she could still the voice that had warned her to hold back. Now she could abandon herself with absolute freedom. He not only loved her but he wished to marry her. She was the most fortunate creature alive.

"I did not think it possible," she murmured as she smoothed her cheek against his.

"Nor did I," he said, revelling in her nearness, "but it appears you are the sort of young lady one marries and, besides, I have rather got used to thinking of you as my bride. I could not possibly give you up now."

"I mean that I did not think you could give up all your many and various ladies for me."

His hand wandered along her arm to her neck. "Whatever do you mean, 'give up all my ladies?'"

"Naturally, you will lose interest in your other ladies."

The smile he wore told her that he contemplated no such step. "I fail to see why one thing logically follows from the other." His amusement was as charming as his smile.

She explained brightly, "I simply assumed that if you love me and wish to marry me, you mean to be faithful to me."

"Of course, I *mean* to be faithful, my dearest, but even the best of intentions may be undermined by temptation. You have seen how little I am able to resist temptation. Indeed, such resistance might well be immoral on my part. For such a man as myself, it goes against nature, and whatever goes against nature is immoral. I have always maintained that my first wish is never to do anything immoral."

Though his words were spoken lightly, she weighed them heavily, and though they were spoken with his usual insouciance, they hurt. His inability to declare his intention to be faithful wounded her sorely, despite the fact that it was exactly what she had always expected of him.

What was she to do? This was the man who meant more to her than life. Now that he had said he loved her and wanted her as his wife, how could she turn away? Unhappily she rested her head against his breast.

With his available arm, he stroked her hair. "I do love you," he said.

"Very well, I will marry you, Roderick," she said numbly.

At this, he exhaled in gratification. Then he raised her lips to his so that he might kiss her again. This time, he did not intend to leave her any breath. When, after a considerable time, he moved his lips to her hair, she held to him tightly.

"I shall not demand fidelity," she vowed in a voice that quavered, as though she faced the guillotine instead of marriage to the man she adored.

Tenderly putting his lips to her eyes, he murmured, "Why are we speaking of infidelity, my love? I am not the least bit weary of you. I haven't even begun to know you, and I wish to know every last inch."

Biting back tears, she declared, "I wish you to know that I shall never interfere with your liaisons."

He was too occupied with inhaling her scent to reply.

"Only promise me, Roderick, you will not expect me to indulge in liaisons of my own. I don't think I should like it."

Abruptly, he held her at arm's length with his unencumbered arm and asked, "Liaisons of your own?"

"I know it is all the crack among the fashionable set for husband and wife to live without what is called 'interference' from the other, and I suppose as Countess of Silverthorne, I shall be expected to engage in as many amours as are consistent with my new station in life. However, you must not insist upon it, Roderick. I know myself too well, and though I love you with all my heart, I could not do it."

He tried to imagine Lucy clinging to the arm of a tulip of fashion at the opera. He tried to picture her behaving in the manner of Miranda Crowther-Biggs, Mrs. Crowther-Biggs and Cora St. John. He tried to see her flirting with any number of beaux, using the very techniques of flirting he had taught her, using them adorably. Try as he might, he could not summon up such images, any more than Lucy could. And he was more glad of it than he could say.

"My dearest," he whispered, "you do not ask me to go against my character in promising fidelity. Therefore, I have no right to ask you to go against your character by promising infidelity."

Somehow this reassurance oppressed her all the more. If she had had any hope that he would storm and rant at the very suggestion of his wife's conducting her own liaisons, it was dashed now. If she had had any hope that he would be so pleased with the prospect of having a faithful wife as to promise equal fidelity through all eternity, it, too, was shattered.

She experienced a grey desolation which seemed familiar, as though she had played this scene before. All at once, she recollected her last meeting with Sir Vale. Then, as now, she had allowed herself to love openly and freely. Then, as now, she had come face to face with the discrepancy between the sort of man she loved and the sort she could live with.

"Now that we have settled this matter to everyone's satisfaction," he said, "prepare to be kissed." He pulled her to him.

She neither put her face up to his nor smiled. Instead, she backed away, saying in an unsteady voice, "Oh, Roderick, I have lied. Forgive me."

"That is all to be forgotten," he assured her. "Now that you are to be my betrothed in fact, we must put aside all that nonsense about the Canterbury tale."

"I lied when I agreed to marry you. I should like nothing better, but I cannot do it."

He smiled tenderly. "Do not distress yourself now. Once we are married, there will be time enough to regret it."

"I am not joking. I cannot knowingly promise to live with a husband who does not regard the marriage vows as I do. I thought I could; I wished to in order to please you. But I know myself too well. I should be eaten up with jealousy and sorrow."

It occurred to him that she was serious. Finding that his usual fund of charming words failed him, he regarded her with concern.

His expression made her reproach herself. "I know you think me dreadfully fickle, and I am deeply sorry, but you would not wish to be shackled to such a wife as I shall make. I could not bear to make us both miserable." She moved again to the door.

"Lucy, you cannot cry off. I love you."

She faced him. "I lied when I said I could overlook your liaisons. I love you too much."

He came to her and, taking her by the shoulders, urged, "Why must we determine the future now? Who knows what will happen in years to come? Think of the present. It is all that matters."

"No," she said, shaking her head. "What matters is that I have been taught a hard lesson: it is not in spite of what you are that I love you; it is because of what you are. Therefore I have neither the desire nor the right to ask you to be anything else. I should not be happy if you changed. And I should not be happy if we went on as you suggest. There is nothing to be done, Roderick, except to ask you to remember that I love you." Before he could protest, she made her escape from the room.

In the corridor, Lucy would have cried tears if she could have, and would have been grateful for the relief. But she was too exhausted. As soon as she reached her chamber, she told herself, she would give way. In the safety and privacy of her tiny room and hard bed, she would permit her feelings to explode.

But when she reached her chamber, she found Lady Philpott, patiently awaiting her return. The presence of a visitor forced Lucy to restrain her feelings. Stone-faced, she sat down on a chair, while her ladyship treated her to a stern lecture.

"My dear girl, I know you have said that you have no interest in Lord Roderick, but I think you must reconsider now. His admiration for you is so evident that I am obliged to call it by its proper name—love. The gentleman loves you, and if you do not value the love of an earl, the love of a man worth thousands and thousands of pounds a year, the love of a man vainly hunted by scores of women, then you are a most ungrateful girl."

WITH CONSIDERABLE STRENGTH for a man who had recently been shot, Lord Roderick flung the door shut. Irritably he strode to his bed, threw himself upon it and thought of what had just passed. He might go after Lucy; he might bring her back. The force of his kisses would be sure to bring her to her senses. But he had never run after any female in his life, never forced himself upon one or lowered himself to plead. It was, he considered, beneath his dignity to make declarations of fidelity, especially to a female to whom he had just declared what he had never before declared—that he loved her and wished to make her the Countess of Silverthorne.

Any other young lady would have been satisfied to hear such words from him. Why must Lucy demand more? Especially when he was light-headed from the loss of blood and the scent of her hair. Thinking of that scent, he paused.

How on earth was he ever going to put Lucy Bledsoe out of his mind? She affected him as no other female did. She was in his thoughts every minute, and when her image was not before him, it was there on the edge of his consciousness, creating a yearning that would not be reasoned or laughed away.

He was recalled to the present by the sound of the door creaking open. His lips framed the word "Lucy," and he smiled. She's come back, he thought.

Then he saw a strange young woman enter. In silence, he watched as her skirts passed in front of him, then back again. Soon he heard the tinkling of dishes and plate and saw his dinner tray being collected from the chest where Lucy had set it. The lantern that hung from the beam had gone dark. A single candle lit the room.

"Who are you?" he asked.

With a coy expression, the young woman bestowed upon him a graceful curtsy. Her hazel eyes gleamed; her full lips smiled. "I am Sophie, sir."

"Come closer, Sophie." He eyed her closely.

Setting down the tray, she approached.

"I cannot quite see you in this poor light," he whispered. "I think you must be very pretty."

"Oh, yes, my lord. Everyone says I am very pretty." She knelt by the bed so that he might see her face, which was indeed as pretty a face as England had ever produced. "Thank you for a most refreshing sight," he said and, moving his wounded arm, grimaced with exaggerated pain.

"Let me assist your lordship," Sophie cooed. Thereupon she slipped an arm behind his back, endeavouring to help him sit up. With her other arm, she reached across his chest to catch a pillow that threatened to fall to the floor.

He smiled at her as her cheek nearly touched his. "You had best be on your guard, Sophie. I am a very sick fellow, but not sick enough, I'm afraid, to keep you safe."

She giggled. "Lawks, the likes of you never frighten me," she said. "To be sure, you are a very fine gentleman, who wears cravats of silk and coats of superfine. To be sure, a gentleman such as yourself would not leave a public house without offering a poor girl something for her trouble."

"I am famous for offering girls something for their trouble. If I can get out of this bed, I shall endeavour to locate my purse."

"I shall assist you, my lord, so that you may find it without delay."

He moaned just audibly enough on his brief walk to the cabinet so that Sophie was obliged to support him with her rosy arms. He found several coins, placed them in the maid's open hand, and permitted her to express her gratitude with a smacking kiss on his cheek. Her lovely face beamed as she stashed the coins in the pocket of her apron and put her arms about his lordship to assist him on his return to his bed.

"Ah, my sweet chambermaid, you are the very medicine I have been wanting," he said. "You do not care for such nonsense as love, marriage or fidelity. You care only for money. I thank you with all my heart."

Pouting, she replied, "You do me an injustice, sir. I like your fine looks very well, I do. I like a man as is handsome. A gentleman who is not handsome is tiresome, to be sure."

"I will not object to your calling me handsome, so long as you do not call me 'husband.' "

"Lawks! What a brazen girl I should be to call a man of your station by such a name. And now, shall I climb in beside you, sir, or do you wish to see my petticoats?"

He regarded her appreciatively, thinking that at last he was faced with a dilemma he knew how to deal with.

LADY PHILPOTT'S DISQUISITION on the charms of Lord Roderick threatened to last until the announcement of supper. "You need not be afraid of failing to get a proposal out of the gentleman," her ladyship declared. "It is true that no one has ever heard of his proposing to a female, but I suspect he may make an exception in your case. He loves you, you see. Now, if you can only bring yourself to overlook his lapses, even so much as a little, I have no doubt we can bring this business to a conclusion by week's end."

Despite her leaden heart, Lucy sat with dignity. "Lady Philpott," she said softly, "the sentiments I felt for Sir Vale Saunders—beginning with love and ending with disillusion—are nothing to what I am experiencing with regard to Lord Roderick at this moment."

Hearing the quaver in Lucy's voice, her ladyship examined her. "You look a little peaked, my dear girl. I daresay, it is all this swoofing about."

Her eyes were still dry and her voice low, but Lucy's emotion could no longer be contained. Trembling she whispered, "I do not see how I am to recover this time, for I not only let down my guard completely, but I lied. I have utterly disregarded my principles, and I am ashamed.''

''Nonsense, my dear girl. Principles are not to be adhered to if they prove inconvenient. Now, to the matter before us. In order to extort an offer of marriage from a man like Lord Roderick, there are certain allurements you must employ. I mentioned them to Susanna Farrineau before she caught Mr. Farrineau, and it is entirely owing to my advice that she caught him at all.''

Turning her head away, Lucy allowed tears to come. She put up her hand to stop her ladyship from saying anything more, for the subject caused her intense anguish. She would have implored Lady Philpott never to mention the earl's name again, but the door opened at that moment with a shattering noise.

To Lucy's astonishment, Lord Roderick entered. He approached, pulled her to a standing position, and said, ''Well, I hope you are pleased with yourself.''

Lady Philpott was too intrigued by his lordship's highly unconventional greeting to raise objections to it. Perhaps she ought to have raised objections, for Lord Roderick wore no shirt, nor any covering whatsoever, upon his chest, the sight of which inspired that widow of many years to blush. Neither did he wear any shoes on his feet. He wore a pair of breeches and not a stitch besides.

The sight of him was painful to Lucy. ''What have I done?'' she asked.

''Do you know who came to my chamber just now?'' he enquired.

Lucy looked at Lady Philpott, who returned her glance with an equal measure of bewilderment. Turning back to Lord Roderick, Lucy answered, "I can't imagine who it was. It could not have been Mr. Turcott, could it? Oh, dear, I hope you are not hurt."

Fixing her with narrowed eyes, he leant against the post which flanked the fireplace, giving both Lucy and her ladyship a view of two fine, strong arms. "Turcott be damned. It was Sophie, the chambermaid."

Again, Lucy tried to find an explanation in Lady Philpott's expression but found only a mirror of her own bafflement. "Sophie, the chambermaid. I hope she did not disturb your rest," she said, for want of anything better to say.

He regarded her with a slight smile. "In point of fact," he said, "I wished her to disturb my rest. And I do not think I boast when I say that she wished to disturb my rest."

It struck Lucy now that his lordship was confessing what she had no wish to hear: that he had made advances to this Sophie, who, apparently, had been more than glad to receive them.

Stung, she studied him, unable to imagine why he should come to tell her such a thing, unless, of course, he meant to reproach her, or arouse her jealousy, or bring home to her what she had lately renounced. If that was his intention, Lucy thought, he had succeeded admirably. She was more than reproached, more than jealous; her heart sank to think of what she had given up. Nevertheless, she took a deep breath and said with as much calm as she could muster, "I suppose she is very pretty."

"Oh, yes, very pretty," he said ruefully.

"Such creatures are always very pretty," Lady Philpott added with a sigh.

Lucy felt so tense that if anyone had touched her, she would have given off sparks. Thus, when she saw Lord Roderick smile at her, a smile of dazzling and consummate roguishness, she did not know what to make of it.

"She was very pretty," he told her softly, "but it all came to nothing. You see, she had one fatal flaw."

"She was not at liberty?"

"She was not *you*."

Suddenly, she grew warm and had to put her hands to her cheeks to cool them. A confusion of feelings overcame her, but one sensation was perfectly clear: she was immensely grateful to Sophie the chambermaid. Indeed, she would not forget, when she left the Blandish Arms Inn, Hostelry and Public House, to make the delightful girl a generous present. Of all the creatures in the world, she liked none better than a chambermaid; none, that is, except the Earl of Silverthorne, who looked at her with such love and laughter that she wished Lady Philpott would see how superfluous was her continued presence in the room.

"Lucy," he said forthrightly, "let us take each other exactly as we are. What do you say? Is it a bargain?" He held out his hand to her.

She smiled, placing her hand in his. "Perhaps we ought to elope. I am awfully good, you know, at planning elopements."

The glow of her eyes, her riveting blue eyes, brought Roderick closer until his nose nearly touched hers. Reaching with his one good arm behind her head, he drew her to him and brought his lips down on hers. For some time, he savoured her kisses until an insistent rap on his arm—his sore arm—recalled him painfully to the present.

Lady Philpott pushed him and Lucy apart to stand between them. "I must remind you, you are not engaged, except in a purely fictional sort of way, and fictional engagements cannot be regarded as binding, at least not for our purposes. You must exchange a promise to marry, and I shall act as witness."

Gladly, they made their promises. Almost as gladly, Lady Philpott witnessed them with her own eyes and ears. The matter concluded to her satisfaction, she discreetly left the lovers to themselves and went to write the great news to Lady Roderick, Lady Knatchbull, and all of London.

EPILOGUE

A MONTH AFTER THE NUPTIALS of the Earl of Silver-thorne and Miss Lucy Bledsoe, Mr. Turcott was kicked in the head by a horse. He subsequently died, thus voiding those contracts which gave him power over Mrs. St. John's fortune.

Mrs. St. John, restored to her position as an eligible widow, was free to accept one of the many proposals of marriage which had been offered her during her stay in the West Indies. Having learned a good deal about men and a good deal about herself, the lady declined all offers of matrimony and, instead, put her fortune to use in the importing and exporting trade under the guidance of Mr. Marlowe, with whom she joined in vigorous public opposition to the slave trade.

Six months after Roderick and Miss Bledsoe exchanged marriage vows, Owen Hunt took to wed Miss Miranda Crowther-Biggs. Although she proved a complaining, selfish wife, Owen was too happy to know it. His mother-in-law gave him as much cause to fret as Lord Roderick had ever done, for she formed a liaison with a dandy half her age, provoking a good deal of malicious talk, not to mention envy.

One year after the wedding of the earl and the young lady whose heart had been broken in Bath, the Farrineaus and Mr. Marlowe returned to England in time for Susanna to present her husband with an heir.

Mr. Marlowe vowed he had never seen a more precocious boy in his life, nor one who was more likely to earn a knighthood for feats of glory or be hanged for acts of mischief. In his nobility, the boy was said to resemble his father, while in his propensity to misbehave, he clearly took after his mother.

Some years after the banns were read for Roderick and Lucy, Lady Philpott declared herself weary of marrying off young girls to the best catches in the Empire. She decided to employ her expertise in her own service. To that end, she made a lengthy visit to Worcestershire so that she might enchant Mr. Marlowe. Indeed, she is in Worcestershire at this very moment, where it is said that the gentleman cannot hold out against her much longer.

Long after his marriage to Lucy, Lord Roderick took advantage of a fine evening to stroll the gardens at Queenscroft. These spacious, rolling grounds, unfettered by walls, were brightened here and there by rectangles of purple, yellow and pink flowers, looking hazy in the twilight. He knew he would find his wife among the roses. To the roses, therefore, he made his way.

Lucy smiled when she saw him approach, but before she could greet him, he put a finger to her lips. "Do not say a word," he warned her. "We must not be discovered."

"There is only Jim the gardener," Lucy said, "and he has gone to get his supper."

Glancing around to see whether they were observed, he said, "It is not Jim I wish to elude. It is your husband."

Calmly, she inspected the bud of a flower. "I do not see why you should wish to elude my husband, who is one of the most estimable gentlemen in Kent, nay, in all the kingdom. If you do not believe me, you may ask his mother."

He bent to sniff the very same rose that she sniffed. "He is also reputed to be extraordinarily handsome," the earl said.

Their eyes met over the blossom. "Yes, he is," she replied. "Our children are fortunate in favouring him."

"I have also heard," he continued in a conspiratorial voice, "that he is a very model of a husband, father, son, landowner and peer of the realm."

Standing upright, Lucy gave a contented nod. "All of that is true, sir, as he will be the first to tell you." She moved to a bush laden with lush pink blooms.

He followed close behind her. "But you cannot be happy with such a fellow, not a remarkable female such as yourself."

"Oh, I think I can be very happy with such a fellow," she said. Then, as though confiding a secret, she whispered, "He is very amusing." Finding herself near a marble bench, she sat down and breathed in the freshness of the summer evening.

He sat next to her and solemnly shook his head. "On the contrary, your husband sounds devilishly dull."

"How can you say so?" she protested earnestly. "He is nothing of the sort."

"He must be dull, for it is said everywhere that he never leaves Queenscroft unless forced to, that on such occasions he always travels with his family, and that he will not even open his London house for two months, so attached is he to his home and hearth."

"Yes," Lucy agreed with pleasure, "and no one is more surprised at such an outcome than I."

"Surely you must find such a fellow wearisome."

"Must I?"

"Surely you must long to be made love to by a gentleman of a bold, adventurous stamp, a gentleman such as myself, who would court you in the manner befitting a woman of your warmth and beauty." Here he seized her hand and held it to his breast.

"That is a highly improper suggestion, sir," she reproved gently. "Pray continue."

On that invitation, he untied her wide-brimmed straw bonnet and put it aside. "I can see I must unfetter you from the constraints of marriage to a dullard."

"You have aroused my curiosity," she confessed, aware that he stroked her hand with breathtaking softness, "but I cannot imagine what you have in view."

"Madam, I am happy to give you further details." Unbuttoning her pelisse, not hurrying the procedure, he said, "Once I have chased that fellow's image from your head, I shall plant my own there." He eased his hands inside the pelisse and round her waist. Then he gave her a light, lingering kiss.

"Your argument is most persuasive," she murmured. "I suppose it is because you studied philosphy at Oxford."

He took her face in his hands. "Then you will meet me tonight at midnight?"

"Yes."

"And you will not tell your husband?"

"I'm afraid I must tell him. I tell him everything."

"He will call me out, I expect."

"Oh, never."

He held her away. "But I am violently in love with you. I intend to run away with you and live with you all the rest of my days. Naturally, he will object to such a plan."

She moved close to him so that he might wrap his arms about her waist once more. "No," she assured him. "He will go to any length to ensure my happiness."

"He sounds a very singular fellow." Here he induced her to rise from the bench so that they stood close, their bodies touching.

Her hands glided along his lapel until they met behind his head. With her lips brushing his, she whispered, "You are quite right. My husband is indeed singular. You see, he is a man who knows his wife well, and he knows that if there is one thing I cannot possibly do, it is resist the charms of a scoundrel."

Coming soon
to an easy chair near you.

FIRST CLASS is Harlequin's armchair travel plan for the incurably romantic. You'll visit a different dreamy destination every month from January through December without ever packing a bag. No jet lag, no expensive air fares and *no* lost luggage. Just First Class Harlequin Romance reading, featuring exotic settings from Tasmania to Thailand, from Egypt to Australia, and more.

FIRST CLASS romantic excursions guaranteed! Start your world tour in January. Look for the special **FIRST CLASS** destination on selected Harlequin Romance titles—there's a new one every month.

NEXT DESTINATION:
THAILAND

 Harlequin Books

JTR2

HARLEQUIN'S "BIG WIN"
SWEEPSTAKES RULES & REGULATIONS

NO PURCHASE NECESSARY TO ENTER OR RECEIVE A PRIZE

1. To enter and join the Reader Service, scratch off the metallic strips on all your BIG WIN tickets #1-#6. This will reveal the values for each sweepstakes entry number, the number of free book(s) you will receive and your free bonus gift as part of our Reader Service. If you do not wish to take advantage of our Reader Service but wish to enter the Sweepstakes only, scratch off the metallic strips on your BIG WIN tickets #1-#4. Return your entire sheet of tickets intact. Incomplete and/or inaccurate entries are ineligible for that section or sections of prizes. Not responsible for mutilated or unreadable entries or inadvertent printing errors. Mechanically reproduced entries are null and void.

2. Whether you take advantage of this offer or not, your Sweepstakes numbers will be compared against the list of winning numbers generated at random by the computer. In the event that all prizes are not claimed by March 31, 1992, a random drawing will be held from all qualified entries received from March 30, 1990 to March 31, 1992, to award all unclaimed prizes. All cash prizes (Grand to Sixth), will be mailed to the winners and are payable by check in U.S. funds. Seventh prize will be shipped to winners via third-class mail. These prizes are in addition to any free, surprise or mystery gifts that might be offered. Versions of this sweepstakes with different prizes of approximate equal value may appear at retail outlets or in other mailings by Torstar Corp. and its affiliates.

3. The following prizes are awarded in this sweepstakes: ★ Grand Prize (1) $1,000,000; First Prize (1) $25,000; Second Prize (1) $10,000; Third Prize (5) $5,000; Fourth Prize (10) $1,000; Fifth Prize (100) $250; Sixth Prize (2,500) $10; ★ ★ Seventh Prize (6,000) $12.95 ARV.

   ★ This presentation offers a Grand Prize of a $1,000,000 annuity. Winner will receive $33,333.33 a year for 30 years without interest totalling $1,000,000.

   ★ ★ Seventh Prize: A fully illustrated hardcover book published by Torstar Corp. Approximate retail value of the book is $12.95.

   Entrants may cancel the Reader Service at anytime without cost or obligation to buy (see details in center insert card).

4. This Sweepstakes is being conducted under the supervision of an independent judging organization. By entering this Sweepstakes, each entrant accepts and agrees to be bound by these rules and the decisions of the judges, which shall be final and binding. Odds of winning in the random drawing are dependent upon the total number of entries received. Taxes, if any, are the sole responsibility of the winners. Prizes are nontransferable. All entries must be received at the address printed on the reply card and must be postmarked no later than 12:00 MIDNIGHT on March 31, 1992. The drawing for all unclaimed sweepstakes prizes will take place May 30, 1992, at 12:00 NOON, at the offices of Marden-Kane, Inc., Lake Success, New York.

5. This offer is open to residents of the U.S., the United Kingdom, France and Canada, 18 years or older, except employees and their immediate family members of Torstar Corp., its affiliates, subsidiaries, and all other agencies and persons connected with the use, marketing or conduct of this sweepstakes. All Federal, State, Provincial and local laws apply. Void wherever prohibited or restricted by law. Any litigation within the Province of Quebec respecting the conduct and awarding of a prize in this publicity contest must be submitted to the Régie des loteries et courses du Québec.

6. Winners will be notified by mail and may be required to execute an affidavit of eligibility and release, which must be returned within 14 days after notification or an alternative winner will be selected. Canadian winners will be required to correctly answer an arithmetical skill-testing question administered by mail, which must be returned within a limited time. Winners consent to the use of their names, photographs and/or likenesses for advertising and publicity in conjunction with this and similar promotions without additional compensation. For a list of major winners, send a stamped, self-addressed envelope to: WINNERS LIST, c/o Harlequin Reader Service, 3010 Walden Ave., P.O. Box 1396, Buffalo, NY 14269-1396. Winners Lists will be fulfilled after the May 30, 1992 drawing date.

If Sweepstakes entry form is missing, please print your name and address on a 3" ×5" piece of plain paper and send to:

In the U.S.	In Canada
Harlequin's "BIG WIN" Sweepstakes	Harlequin's "BIG WIN" Sweepstakes
3010 Walden Ave.	P.O. Box 609
P.O. Box 1867	Fort Erie, Ontario
Buffalo, NY 14269-1867	L2A 5X3

Offer limited to one per household.

© 1991 Harlequin Enterprises Limited   Printed in the U.S.A.

LTY-H191R